e-luv

e-luv
an Internet romance

Dave Roberts

FRIDAY
BOOKS

First published in Great Britain in 2006 by Friday Books
An imprint of The Friday Project Limited
83 Victoria Street, London SW1H 0H
www.thefridayproject.co.uk
www.fridaybooks.co.uk

British Library Cataloguing in Publication Data.
A catalogue record for this book is available
from the British Library.

ISBN 10 – 0 954 83188 8
ISBN 13 – 9 780 9548318 8 2

Designed and produced by Staziker Jones
www.stazikerjones.co.uk

The Publisher's policy is to use paper manufactured
from sustainable forests.

To the Roberts family –
Edward, Gertrud, Miriam, Hazel, Bill, Frank and Liz.

Acknowledgements

Thanks to Birrell for the advice and encouragement, David Hayes for his ideas and for keeping me going, Kevin Cummins for the suggestions and interweb expertise, Mike Coulter for the computer, Nick Frost for his inspirational work on multi-agency working, Angie for being Angie (as well as one of the characters in this book) and Ian Davies for sharing his knowledge on poker.

About the Author

Dave Roberts (dave@stripeyjumper.com) left his end terrace in Chorlton-Cum-Hardy in 1982 to seek fame and fortune in New Zealand. Despite failing spectacularly on both counts, he made a living out of advertising before illness cut his career short. Being housebound meant the internet played an unnaturally big part in his daily routine, which revolved around chatrooms, eBay, online gambling and time-wasting sites. Whilst these things are no longer part of his life, they gave him the inspiration to write *e-luv*, which is based on his online experiences.

🖤 Introduction

There are a few things you should know about Internet romances.

The statements 'I've never felt this way about anyone before' and 'It's like we've known each other our entire lives' will be used time and again.

You will find yourself typing things you'd never dream of saying to a fellow human being in real life. For example, 'As I look out of the window, I can see a bright star. Every time I look at it, I will think of you.'

In cyberspace no one can see you squirm.

Everyone pretends to have no interest in physical appearance. 'It's what's inside that counts,' you find yourself saying. Followed, a few sentences later, by 'So...what do you look like?'

You'll make plans for the future. You'll tell the object of your affection that you want to grow old with them. You'll tell them how much you miss them when they go away for a few days. You'll proclaim undying love.

Then, with a bit of luck, you'll get to meet them.

And that's usually when it falls apart.

This is the story of three years of Internet relationships. The dozens of women (well, I presume they were women) I wrote to, talked to, met up with and, in two cases, moved in with.

It all started on a summer night in 1999...

Chapter 1

 Wed 7.20 pm

'What do you look like?'

If you're a female in a chatroom, it's only a matter of time before you see this sentence appear on your screen.

It's like your average adolescent male is expecting a bevy of supermodels to be sitting in front of their computers, scantily clad and hanging around in chatrooms.

But where else could the painfully shy, the socially inept and the hideously ugly become a babe magnet?

Here was I, virtually housebound through an illness that had the doctors baffled, zero social life, overweight, broke, unemployed and soon to be homeless. I'd just spent the last of my money on a computer (wasting it on the mortgage seemed pointless, since I was so far behind). The Internet seemed a magnificent way of passing the long drawn-out New Zealand summer days, filling that seemingly endless void between waking and falling asleep.

I'd read about cyber romances, of course. There was a story in the news about a local man who had started talking to an American woman a couple of weeks earlier, and had already decided to donate his kidney – yes, his kidney – so that she could live a long and happy life with him.

I found such desperation endearing. This was clearly a man who had not enjoyed a great deal of success with the opposite sex.

I could relate to him.

While I wasn't quite ready to donate my kidney to the first semi-attractive woman to come along, I was willing to negotiate.

My first chatroom was called Paris. For those unfamiliar with chatrooms, they're basically places where up to thirty or so people can type messages to each other.

I went in under the pseudonym Lord Brett Sinclair, a name intended to convey my grasp of subtle irony, since Lord Brett was a characterplayed by Roger Moore in an unconvincing 1970s TV series, *The Persuaders.*

As I was soon to learn, people thought either I was (a) someone pretending to be a real life lord of the realm, or (b) a real life lord of the realm.

Once inside the chatroom, I scanned the names of my fellow chatters.

One name immediately caught my eye. Not because it was particularly good, but because of the eccentric spelling.

Her name was Lady Gwinnivear.

My fingers seemed to take on a life of their own, as they typed out things my brain would never even consider.

 Thu 11.32 am

'How art thou, m'lady?' I found myself saying.

A couple of minutes later, long after I'd given up on any hope of a reply, one arrived.

'I am well, my lord. And thoust?'

I wasn't entirely convinced the knights of old used the word 'thoust', but carried on regardless, with the time-honoured questions.

'Where art thou from, fair lady?'

Five minutes later:

'Sorry...had to feed the dog, then some asshole came to the door and tried to sell me frigging insurance. Anyways, I'm from Delacroix, Louisiana. Where art thou from m'lord?'

'I am from the fair city of Oxford, England, but living in Wellington, New Zealand, due to a misunderstanding with various credit card companies,' I replied. *'May I gently enquire your age?'*

'Twenty-six,' she replied. *'And thoust?'*

Obviously, I had to lie. So I did, by knocking a few years off. My next question probably didn't catch her by surprise.

'So...what dost thou look like?'

'How about I send a photo? I'll do it if you tell me what you look like.'

'You've got yourself a deal. Well, I'm about 5' 10", weigh around 200 pounds, grey hair, big nose, hazel eyes. Someone once said I look like an English professor.'

'You know what you sound like, m'lord?'

'No.'

'You sound like my kinda guy.'

 # Fri 1.12 pm

If that little exchange made my ego soar, a visit from my insurance agent that evening sent it plummeting back down again. He'd come to discuss my policy, which I wanted to cash in so I could pay some bills.

He fixed me with a practised gaze, taking in my unkempt shock of more-white-than-grey hair, which hadn't been cut in years, my pasty skin, which hadn't seen the sun for about the same amount of time, and my tired, flabby body, which had long ceased being a well-toned source of pride.

'If I were you, I'd keep the policy going until you reach retirement. I mean, what are you now, fifty-seven, fifty-eight?'

I just nodded in agreement, too embarrassed to tell him the truth – that it was a few weeks after my thirty-ninth birthday.

 # Fri 9.22 pm

By the time Lady Gwinnivear's photo arrived (via e-mail), I'd learnt a few more things about her. She was an 'exotic dancer' and was on the run from an abusive husband (this was to become a familiar tale). Her real name was Jacqui and she had a young daughter, Courtney.

Her family redefined the word 'dysfunctional'. An almost impossible-to-follow labyrinth of cruel stepfathers, a heartless mother, and assorted other relatives who cared little or nothing for her.

Her view of the British came entirely from the film *Braveheart*. I don't think she expected us all to wander around in kilts and facepaint, but she was very upset with me over the barbaric mistreatment of William Wallace.

When I pointed out that this was hardly my fault, she answered brilliantly with, *'Well, of course you're going to say that. Although I'm not saying it was your fault* per se.*'*

She used the phrase *per se* in almost every e-mail and conversation.

As for the photo, it showed a glamorous blonde who was way out of my league. This was the type of woman who wouldn't even notice me if there were just the two of us stuck in a lift together.

She was gorgeous. And, what's more, we seemed to be enjoying each other's conversation.

We discussed music, and she said she was going to send me a tape of her favourites. The fact that this included the likes of *Queensryche*, *Poison* and *Whitesnake* didn't alarm me as much as it should've done. After all, we couldn't have everything in common, could we?

By now we were talking for several hours a day, sometimes up to three or four. It did occur to me once or twice that she didn't seem to spend a lot of time exotic dancing, but I banished the thought as soon as it came. In the Internet world, it's important to believe what you want to believe. And right now, I was wanting to believe that a beautiful young stripper was hopelessly in love with me.

 Tue 5.36 pm

I'd also started talking to Petra, an Australian in her mid-twenties, who was incredibly enthusiastic about, well, everything.

She was telling me about her latest Internet romance.

'He's totally incredible,' she gushed. *'He's already a pro golfer at twenty-four, and apparently he's being talked about as the next Tiger Woods. I've never felt this way about anyone before. It's like we've known each other our entire lives.'*

I'd actually talked to this chap in the chatroom before. He was Irish, and everyone I mentioned, he'd been drinking with recently. The list included Peter O'Toole, Bob Geldof and Bono from *U2*.

He'd also told Petra about how he broke the course record the previous week, and that it was all down to her. I saw the e-mail he sent her. It described how he was walking down the fairway on the final hole, clutching a pendant she'd sent.

'*Petra, darling,*' he whispered to himself, '*I'm doing this for you.*'

He then went and made his putt, and the gallery erupted. On the TV interview afterwards, he explained how it was all down to this lovely Aussie lass.

Of course, he would've sent her a video, he explained. But would you believe it – he forgot to set the tape.

He also told her that he'd decided to forgo the European golf season and play in Australia instead, just so he could be with her.

Because he was already independently wealthy, they wouldn't have to worry about money. He'd take care of her.

Petra was besotted. And since his birthday was imminent, she decided to make something special for him: a montage of his greatest golfing triumphs. She searched the Internet for mentions of him.

And found none.

Even then, she didn't suspect a thing.

Nor did she suspect a thing when a friend of his rang her, a week before he was due to arrive, saying the love of Petra's life had injured himself in a freak accident and wouldn't be able to make it.

Apparently, he was working at the golf shop, and sliced his arm open, rupturing the tendon.

She immediately rang every hospital in Dublin, but none had heard of him.

A few weeks later, he admitted to her that he'd lied about pretty much everything, and was off to England to meet up with a sixteen-year-old girl he'd met on the Internet.

 Fri 3.20 am

It was around three in the morning when the phone rang.

'Hi, honey,' purred an unfamiliar American female. 'It's your Lady Gwinnivear. I just had to hear your voice.'

I'm really not at my best at three in the morning. All the smooth lines and casual-yet-excruciatingly-witty repartee I'd planned were nowhere to be found.

'Oh, hi,' I yawned.

'Oh, honey, I didn't wake you, did I?'

'No, no...it's okay.' Then, as consciousness flooded back, I got straight down to important matters.

'So, m'lady, may I enquire as to what thou art wearing?'

She giggled.

'Well, wouldn't you like to know?'

'So...?'

'Okay, so I'm wearing a yellow T-shirt, shorts and white cotton panties. How's about you?'

'Me? Not a stitch, m'lady.'

(Totally untrue, but the hideous, food-stained striped pyjama bottoms and old T-shirt with *Ponch from CHiPS* on it didn't quite have the erotic imagery I was striving for.)

 # Sat 8.48 am

Next morning, I switched on the computer and eagerly checked my e-mail.

There, amongst the *'You have been specially selected to get Viagra at a fraction of the usual cost'* offers, was a little note from Jacqui.

It told, in graphic detail, about how she released her pent-up frustration after getting turned on talking to me.

Now, even though I was new to the computer, I knew that I'd be able to forward her e-mail to a couple of my (real-life) friends so that they'd be able to see what a stud I was.

So I attached it, together with a note that read:

Only met this chick yesterday. Yank...but aren't they all? She's gorgeous, young, blonde, blue eyes, big tits...what more could you want? I'm going to ask her for some nude pics and will pass them on as soon as they arrive.

Trevor

I then sent it off and sat back, waiting for words of envy to come winging back from my pals.

It was only as I was drifting into an erotic daydream that I realised something wasn't quite right. You know how in films people sit bolt upright when they realise something awful's happened?

Well, I sat bolt upright – and sank my head in my hands.

I'd sent the mail not to my friends, but clicked Reply, instead.

Which meant I'd sent it to Jacqui.

Sun 10.02 pm

As I was telling my online friend Scott about this disaster, he (in attempting to make me feel better) told me about his most humiliating moment.

He'd been chatting to this girl Tara from Los Angeles for about a year. They were so serious about each other that they had already chosen names for their children, and looked at houses via real estate sites on the Internet.

They hadn't actually met, but that was a mere formality.

He claimed to be one of the few males who genuinely don't care about looks, and she, being a modern, non-judgemental woman, found appearance to be an irrelevance, foisted upon society by an image-obsessed media.

I'd seen her photo, and could understand why she'd feel this way.

Anyway, after running up huge phone bills, they decided to move in together. She still had a year left at school, so it was decided that he'd come to her and get a job – any kind of job. The important thing was that they could be together.

Now I know what you're thinking. How could they think about living together when they hadn't even met? Well, as a veteran of Internet romances, I understand perfectly. You can easily fall in love, although I'm still not sure whether you fall for the actual person, or for an idealised version.

Scott flew out to LA straight after he'd worked the last day at his job. Tara had found an apartment for them and had already moved in. They'd live there for a few months, taking their time to find their dream home.

The first meeting had been discussed many times. They had agreed that they would immediately embrace and enjoy that first kiss. The kiss that both had waited over a year to savour.

Sadly, it didn't work out like that. As soon as she saw him, she ran away.

Scott spent the next few days trying to find her, before flying home a sadder yet wiser man.

 **Sat 11.01 pm**

The phone rang.

'Trevor, it's Jacqui.'

I knew I was in trouble. This was the first time she hadn't called me by my aristocratic pseudonym.

'God, it's great to hear your voice,' I gushed, desperately wondering how I was going to get out of this mess.

'You wanna explain this e-mail you sent me?' she demanded.

The only thing I could think of was incredibly weak. However, I had no option. I had to give it a try.

'Oh, that? Just my little joke, honey. I sent it to you on purpose. Don't tell me you thought... Oh, m'lady... I feel terrible now.'

'Oh, m'lord, I am so relieved. I didn't think you were serious *per se*, but it kinda upset me.'

Like I said before, on the Internet it's important to believe what you want to believe.

Jacqui's phone calls were becoming quite frequent. It felt like an enjoyable version of being stalked.

I could tell it was her when I was greeted with an appallingly bad English accent, saying, 'I say, old chap,' or 'What ho! Jolly good show, what?'

Hollywood has a lot to answer for.

We sent each other little gifts, like the music tapes.

I played mine once. Ghastly. I think she felt the same way about hers, but was too polite to say. It was designed to show her how hip I was, with unlistenable experimental jazz combined with unlistenable loud, obnoxious punk.

Even I couldn't listen to it, so I have no idea how she could.

One night, as we chatted away in the chatroom, she asked if I wanted to cyber.

'*Cyber? What do you mean?*' I typed.

'*You know, honey – have cybersex.*'

 Wed 4.57 pm

Anna was another chat friend, and, like most of us, she was in love with someone she'd never met. Or even spoken to.

He was a forty-seven-year-old artist and DJ from Toronto. She particularly liked the fact that he'd brought up his two children single-handedly, after being widowed at a relatively early age.

His picture showed a handsome, dignified man, with kind eyes and a sweet smile.

Sometimes his communication skills weren't all she could have wished for, but this was, as she explained, *'because French is his first language and his typing is poor'*.

One day, she was discussing Internet romances with another woman, Princess Aurora. She showed Aurora her man's picture, and was surprised when there was no response.

A few minutes later, the same picture appeared on screen. From Princess Aurora.

It seemed that the same man was carrying on with both of them. And then things took a bizarre twist.

Yet another person in the chatroom recognised the picture. It was a publicity still of an actor from a cable network vampire soap opera.

Anna got the chatroom owner to trace the address of the person who'd sent it.

The forty-seven-year-old artist and DJ turned out to be an eighteen-year-old college girl from a small town in Oklahoma.

Evidently, life in Oklahoma is very, very dull.

Wed 10.55 am

Jacqui had concocted a typically complex medieval fantasy world in which I was to lose my cybervirginity.

'I am Lady Gwinnivear,' she typed, *'and I am locked in a tower by my evil stepfather. M'lord must rescue me, and I shall repay him by doing anything he desires.'*

So, what she was saying is that if I play along with this, I'll get a shag. Or a cybershag, which isn't quite as good. In fact, it's basically wanking in front of a grey box, reading words on the screen.

'*Very well, m'lady,*' I began. '*I have followed your trail to the castle, which is heavily guarded, surrounded by a moat and has the drawbridge up.*'

'*What's a moat, m'lord?*'

'*Oh, it's a...water thing. So anyway, I overpower one of the guards and steal his uniform. Putting it on, I walk across the drawbridge and into the castle.*'

'*I see you from my windowpane,*' she replied, showing no respect for historical accuracy, '*and lay down on the bed, awaiting your strong arms.*'

Phew! This was more like it. Time to speed things up.

'*I kill all the guards en route, lock your stepfather up and open the door to your chamber.*'

'*I am soooo happy to see you,*' she responded, '*that I clutch you to my ample bosom. I am pleasantly surprised to feel the hardness of your proud manhood.*'

Blimey!

'*M'lady, I am aroused because I have never witnessed such beauty, nor been in the presence of such an epitome of femininity.*'

'*My lord, I tear my clothes off. My red flowing dress and thong are flung away. I want you to take me.*'

'*I grab your tits and squeeze them.*'

'*A bit more gentle, honey.*'

'*Sorry. I gently caress your pale white breasts, kissing your pale soft belly.*'

'*I respond by taking your manhood in my mouth and softly suck it.*'

'*My kisses get lower and lower, and eventually reach your womanhood.*'

Womanhood? Where did that one come from? I carried on regardless.

'*My hands gently stroke your tight buttocks.*'

Hmmm. So one of my hands is caressing her breasts and two of them are stroking her buttocks.

'*M'lord, I want to feel you inside me.*'

'*I ease my stiff manhood gently inside you, and with slow, deliberate strokes slowly build to a crescendo.*'

That's the brilliant thing about cybersex. Whereas in real life, I might last a few minutes, here I can appear to be the kind of stud who can delay orgasm for hours on end.

'M'lord, I can feel my orgasm beginning. It is now overwhelming me. Never have I felt such pleasure.'

'I come inside you, and we lie together, spent, sharing a cigarette.'

'I don't smoke.'

'Well, neither do I. But isn't that what people are supposed to do after sex?'

'M'lord?'

'Yes, sweet lady?'

'Wouldn't it be fun if we could do that in real life? I think we should meet.'

 # Thu 8.03 am

The more disastrous reality became, the more I retreated into cyberlife.

Everything was closing in on me. The building society was leaving daily messages, requesting I get in contact.

The bailiff was a regular visitor, threatening to take my furniture unless I paid various fines.

I was getting recorded voices phoning to say that I had forty-eight hours to pay my phone bill. The electricity people were slightly more generous – they were prepared to wait four days.

The bank was so fed up with bouncing cheques that it eventually stopped informing me.

It was time either to face up to my responsibilities, or go into massive denial.

I chose the latter, and stopped answering the phone, or opening letters in brown envelopes. And I spent longer and longer each day on the Internet.

Sleep was built around global time zones. I had to be awake when the British would be in chatrooms, when the American/Canadian college types got home, and when the Aussies and Kiwis were around.

The optimum time to catch sleep was between two and seven in the morning. The remaining nineteen hours were spent in front of the computer. Jacqui had shown me how easy it was to meet stunning women with a minimum of effort.

In real life, I'd had one date since my marriage had broken up, nearly three years earlier, and it's a memory that haunts me to this day. She was a teacher, and spent nearly forty-five minutes lecturing me on the causes and effects of the El Niño weather pattern. At the end she asked if I had any questions. Really.

The law of averages dictated that with all this time on the Internet, I'd eventually meet someone not only in the same country as me, but also with a few things in common.

I did. And her name was Kate.

Wed 6.33 am

Kate, who lived in Tauranga, a town about 350 miles away, had three things going for her:

1. She was a woman and liked me.
2. She was as desperate as me.
3. She was a corporate caterer, which meant she probably had money.

I hadn't told her about Jacqui. Not because I was trying to hide the fact that I was involved with someone, but because I was trying to hide the fact that I was involved with someone on the Internet, who lived half a world away.

After swapping e-mails for a couple of days, I plucked up the courage to ring her. Now while a couple of days might not sound a long time in the course of a normal relationship, it's enough time, in Internet terms, to meet your soulmate, write long, gushy letters, talk to them on the phone, pledge undying love, have a fight and break up.

Before moving on to the next soulmate.

Kate at least had a healthy dose of cynicism, and I enjoyed talking to her. I still had no idea what she looked like, despite asking almost continuously. The expression she used was that she 'wasn't disappointed with what she'd been given'.

Good enough for me.

We talked about meeting. More specifically, what we were going to do. It was decided that she'd come down to Wellington in three weeks' time for the entire weekend. She'd knock on the door, I'd answer it and we'd make love. Without saying a word to each other. Just do it and then talk.

She told me she was going to whet my appetite for the encounter by sending a couple of photos.

I couldn't believe my luck. A woman actually wanted to have sex with me. And the fact that I was virtually housebound didn't matter. She was coming to me. This was brilliant.

My only problem was the rash. My entire leg was covered in it. Bright red and impossible to miss. As soon as she saw it, she'd run screaming from the house. I know I would in her position. So I tentatively brought up the subject.

'So, Kate...hypothetically, if a chap had a bit of a leg rash, would this be a huge turn off for you? Hypothetically speaking?'

'No, of course not.'

Perfect. I got up the next morning bright and early, awaiting the postman. When the letter finally arrived, I paused before opening it, wondering what she'd look like. From her description, she was a Julia Roberts type, with long, reddish-brown hair, slim figure and sparkling brown eyes. Oh, and lips just made for kissing.

I couldn't wait any longer. I tore open the envelope.

Wed 9.19 am

Jacqui had also sent me a little package, which I opened first. The smell of cheap perfume wafted out, and further investigation revealed a pair of skimpy silk panties, which had been liberally doused in the stuff.

There were also some more photos. Now at this early stage of my Internet life, I hadn't yet learnt that if a woman has had Glamor Shots® taken, alarm bells should ring.

A Glamor Shot®, for the uninitiated, is a soft-focus photograph taken of a woman, usually American, wearing a bizarre array of supposedly sexy outfits. This invariably includes a leather jacket, cowboy shirt and hat, and shiny sequinned dress.

Jacqui had sent three photos. In one she wore a leather jacket. In another she wore a cowboy shirt and hat. While in the last one she wore a shiny sequinned dress.

She looked great. It was only later that I realised any resemblance to any persons, either living or dead, was purely coincidental.

 ## Sat 10.19 am

Kate's photo was a classic illustration of the massive gap between expectation and reality.

She looked very bookish, with a sensible, no-nonsense haircut, sensible, no-nonsense glasses and a stern expression. Not exactly Julia Roberts. Still, I now knew that underneath she was something of a sex goddess and she was always fun to talk to.

She rang later that night.

'It's Kate,' she said, 'and they're blue today.'

I think I may have been getting a bit predictable. I hadn't even asked what colour knickers she was wearing, and here she was telling me.

'My favourite colour, as if you didn't know,' I said, 'and by the way, I got a little something in the post from you this morning.'

'Oh, you got my pic...what did you think?'

'I think you're gorgeous. I also think you should come and visit me next weekend, instead of the weekend after.'

'Oh, you do, do you? And how do you suggest I do this?'

'Just jump on a plane.'

'That'd be the 24th of November, right? Okay, I'll have a think about it and get back to you – and don't forget I want a photo of you!'

Gulp.

Mon 7.20 pm

My two Internet relationships were becoming increasingly divided into the erotic-turned-romantic relationship (Jacqui), and the purely sexual relationship (Kate).

Whereas Jacqui wrote things like:

> *If only you truly knew how I am feeling for you. But I'm still not sure that it wouldn't frighten you away. It's like I feel your soul touching me from this long distance between us. I feel you so close to me, like you're right here.*

Kate would be more likely to send e-mails like:

> *I can't wait to feel your 7-inch cock inside me.*

(Okay, so I exaggerated – but that was before I knew we'd actually meet. I now had to find a way to explain how my penis had lost a couple of inches in a matter of weeks.)

Did I feel guilty about carrying on with two women, which is something I wouldn't dream of doing in real life? Strangely, no. It wasn't until a lot later that I realised that Internet people are real people with real feelings. It may seem obvious, but when you're sitting in front of a computer unable to feel, touch, smell or see a person, they rarely seem more than one-dimensional.

Wed 3.22 pm

Having discovered an endless supply of women on the Internet, I now discovered an endless supply of everything else: eBay.

I was obsessed. In just three weeks, I had accumulated an impressive variety of things I didn't need.

It started harmlessly enough, with a solar-powered alarm clock, developed using NASA technology.

Then, still on a high from winning that auction, I got caught up in a frenzied bidding war for a pair of brown yachting shoes with leather laces. After they became mine, I was feeling invincible.

My next acquisition was an Ab Cruncher, which promised rock-hard abdominal muscles in just three minutes a day. It represented a breakthrough that also utilised NASA technology.

This particular spree came to an end with the purchase of an electric stirfry pan, which apparently had no design input from NASA.

eBay had been a lifesaver, since it meant that I could buy clothes from all over the world without leaving the house.

I wore Diesel jeans from Italy, a Fred Perry shirt from Thailand (although its authenticity was in doubt, since the label read FERD PERRY) and Joseph Siegel shoes from Germany.

All brand new. All at bargain prices.

I was the best-dressed hermit in town.

Mon 9.07 am

'*What are you doing on the 24th?*' asked Jacqui, as we were chatting away in our favourite chatroom.

I froze in panic. Had she somehow found out about Kate's visit?

'*I don't know. Nothing. Why?*'

'*Well, you know that's my birthday? My mom has offered me a flight anywhere I want. I'm thinking about going to Scotland or coming to see my honey.*'

Okay. So now two women were prepared to fly all the way to Wellington, for the express purpose of having sex with a much older, overweight, unemployed couch potato.

What was more, they both wanted to come on the same day.

'*Scotland? Why would you want to go there?*' I asked, trying desperately to give myself time to think.

'*The awesome history,*' she explained. '*I want to see William Wallace's grave. Well, not his grave per se, but the place he was buried. Look at the places he fought and stuff.*'

'*And why would you want to come and see me?*' I asked, casually fishing for compliments.

'*I love you.*'

Whaaaaaat?

'*I love you and I know you love me. You're not that easy to read, Trevor. But I feel your love through the cosmos to me even though you're afraid to admit it. I know you do. But it does frighten you a tad. It's OK, darling. I told you I'd never push it.*'

Christ! And there was me thinking I had found one of the few stable people on the Internet. Now I was totally out of my depth. I tried to change the subject.

'*So...you like flying?*'

It didn't work.

'*You make me feel so good. Like a woman, not an object like most men do. You see me for who I am. That is trust.*'

'Oh. Good.'

'*You are so special, Trevor. God knows, if I had wings, I'd fly to you now. You're such a beautiful spirit and I can't believe no other woman has seen that in you.*'

I was left with the feeling she was perfectly capable of turning up on my doorstep at any time, unannounced.

 # Thu 12.00 pm

The great thing about my Internet womanising was that they couldn't see how ill I was. I suppose I was hoping (rather like the spotty kid who sits alone in the corner, smiling to himself) that someone would notice me for my gorgeous wit and personality to such an extent that they'd be willing to overlook the physical flaws.

I had mixed feelings about Kate coming down. On one hand, I was terrified of having to interact with a real person and try to appear normal. On the other hand, I wanted a shag.

It was a couple of days before she was due to arrive that I decided to arrange a little insurance. I planned a chatroom marathon, where I intended meeting several women with whom I could have cyberaffairs if the Kate thing was, as I anticipated, an unmitigated disaster.

We talked on the phone every night, as soon as she got home from work. The thought of touching a real, live woman was delicious. I even decided to have a bath in her honour, and wash my hair.

I still wasn't certain that Jacqui wouldn't turn up, and even entertained some threesome fantasies. She wasn't entirely predictable, and the more I learnt about her, the more confusing she became.

At times, she seemed to forget that she was an exotic dancer, and told me about some of the ghastly co-workers at the shop. I didn't bother pointing out such contradictions – after all, I didn't want her to examine some of my claims too closely.

She repeatedly told me that she loved me. And when I didn't reply, she also told me that I loved her too. When I finally admitted to a certain degree of fondness, she replied:

'*Teardrops of joy fill my eyes, flow down my ivory cheeks. I sit here enraptured by you. You must know that.*'

This was getting scary. Particularly when she finished the thought with:

'*You'll never walk alone again. My footprints will be beside yours.*'

I had a feeling that if she found out about Kate, I might well be in trouble.

Chapter 2

 ## Mon 11.18 pm

You know those letters you get, breathlessly offering you credit cards, loans or telling you about exciting new accounts that your bank has come up with? They're packed with information about accounts designed to fit in with your lifestyle. Or plans that would help your savings grow as your family grows. Or cards that reward you simply for using them regularly.

The signature at the end is usually the marketing manager or your personal banker.

But if the letter came from a certain high-profile multinational bank any time in the past twelve years, it was probably written by me.

As a copywriter, I had written letters for six different marketing managers and hundreds of personal bankers. And I hated every minute of it.

It got harder and harder to get enthused about a drop of half a per cent, or an exclusive new platinum credit card designed to reflect the holder's status. When I first became ill, I assumed my employer would stand by me while I got treatment. The doctor had given me some pills that just made me worse, and he'd also told me to get plenty of rest.

I'd been off work for four weeks when I got a letter from Dave Ferris, the marketing manager, who was my immediate boss, telling me that I no longer had a job. He also told me that since I had already been off work for so long, I would not be paid any further salary, and because I had taken sick leave without asking, I was not entitled to the usual one month's notice or any accumulated holiday pay. This left me $3865 out of pocket – money I badly needed.

I wondered who he'd got to write all this for him.

Mon 1.20 pm

Emma, my first (and only) wife, worked at the same bank, but neither of us was aware of the other's existence until we went away together.

She worked a couple of floors above me, doing something that involved foreign exchange, and never had any reason to come down to the marketing department. We only got to meet because we'd both been chosen to go on a team-building course at a windswept collection of log cabins in the middle of nowhere.

From what I could make out, we were the only ones who actually did any bonding, and this stemmed from a shared fear of bungee jumping. When it was announced that everyone was going to have a go, we both wormed our way out by citing non-specific medical reasons.

Since Emma and I were stuck in a cabin together, we got talking, and before we knew it, everyone else had returned after being away for over half a day.

When we got back to civilisation, we went to lunch; lunch became dinner; and dinner became spending the night together. When this became spending the weeks together, it was obvious we were in it for the long run.

I was happy. Emma was not only pretty, with striking blue eyes and a smile that was never far from her lips, but she was also fun to be with. As a bonus, she had her own parking space at work, which meant I got a lift in every day in her brand new 1986 Toyota Corolla.

I think if I hadn't fallen ill, if she hadn't married again, and if she didn't hate me with a passion, we might still be together.

 # Mon 1.55 pm

The elaborate proposal I had worked out wasn't needed because Emma beat me to it.

We were stuck in traffic on the way to work when she noticed that the car in front had 'Just Married' spray-painted over the boot, and empty cans trailing along behind.

'Wonder how long she had to wait before he asked?' she said.

'Dunno. Why?'

'Nothing. It's just that some men are slower than others, that's all.'

Now, I may be slow, but I'm not that slow.

We were married in early 1990. The only depressing thing about the wedding was the number of bank employees in attendance. Not that I've got anything against them particularly, just that I've never seen myself as one of them.

We were determined not to get any old house. It had to be the house of our dreams. An older-style bungalow with plenty of garden, high ceilings and three bedrooms.

We must have looked at fifteen or twenty houses before finding the right one. We knew it was the one before even taking a step inside. It just felt right.

We spent three of the happiest years of my life there, before my illness turned our lives upside down.

I can recall the exact moment our dream home became my prison. It was the day after I'd got the letter from work, and I had been feeling increasingly as though everything was spiralling out of control.

I opened the door to go and collect the milk, but as soon as I took a step outside, I was totally overwhelmed by anxiety. The ground felt as though it was moving in a wave-like motion. My legs had lost all strength. My heart was beating so fast and so loud, I was sure it was going to burst out of my chest. The fear levels were similar to what they would have been had I been dangling over a pool of hungry piranhas.

Slamming the door shut, I somehow found my way to bed and promptly collapsed on it, shaking, feeling faint and totally convinced I was about to die.

I wouldn't take another step outside for nearly four years.

 # Mon 2.40 pm

Emma tried really hard to adapt to me being home all day, and I tried really hard to adapt to her being at work all day.

I was jealous of her because she was leading a normal life, while she was angry with me because she was the only one bringing in any money.

The trouble was that she couldn't see anything wrong with me, and the doctors couldn't actually find anything wrong. The only logical conclusion for her to come to was that there wasn't anything wrong with me.

She grew increasingly frustrated at my inability to function the way I used to. Suddenly, her social life had been taken away from her and we had to forget any plans to have a family.

Eventually, we decided on a trial separation, which is a way of saying you're splitting up when neither of you wants to face up to the fact.

Since I couldn't be the one to leave, she went, taking with her pretty much everything we owned. I insisted on it, to try and stop myself feeling so guilty. I got to stay in the house and pay the mortgage. Then, when I was well enough, we'd sell it and split the proceeds.

And that's how I found myself stuck in a small suburban bungalow with a fridge, sofa, table, bed, wardrobe and rapidly dwindling bank balance.

And, of course, a computer.

Mon 4.23 pm

It wasn't until the mid-1990s that I stopped hiding behind the sofa whenever anyone called round, and it was another couple of years before I could actually leave the house and do my own shopping.

There was no miracle cure. I just pushed myself to do a tiny bit more each day.

I had a comfort zone, which meant I could drive to the local shopping mall, where there was everything I needed (i.e. a supermarket and a post office), with minimum anxiety. I could also get to a restaurant known as the Casablanca Café, which I had been to approximately forty-five times in the past two years – despite the fact that it had large photographs of Humphrey Bogart on the wall.

As for walking, I couldn't get so far. On a good night (agoraphobics don't like going out during the day) I could get to the end of the road, where there was a small minimart.

I still didn't have a social life, but that was probably just as well. By this stage, anything that threatened to interfere with my chat schedule made me just as panicky as the great outdoors.

People talk about Internet addiction as though it's something that might or might not exist, but believe me, it's very real.

There are countless websites devoted to the topic. I should know: I've probably visited each one, usually when there's nobody interesting in any of my favourite chatrooms.

On one site I read about a woman who admitted to spending up to ten hours a day on the Internet, leaving her family to fend for themselves.

I couldn't remember the last day I spent only ten hours online.

It was time I saw a doctor. So as soon as I felt well enough to cope with a visit, I arranged for him to come and see me.

Tue 4.40 pm

I sold the furniture. It made sense. If I didn't sell it, the bailiff would've seized it.

The sofa, kitchen table and wardrobe got enough to pay the mortgage for a month, and left enough over for either the rates bill or a new modem.

No contest. I got a flash, high-speed modem. It meant I could do everything a little faster on the Internet, which would make chatroom life run a lot more smoothly.

I also got my first Internet bill. This was the first time in my life I'd looked at a bill and burst into helpless laughter. $2300. For a month. At $5 an hour, it meant I'd spent over 100 hours every week online.

There was no way I could come up with that kind of money. I wasn't able to work, and recovery didn't feel like it was imminent.

My doctor didn't have a clue what was wrong with me. The symptoms didn't fit anything he'd ever come across. It just felt as though most of my brain had closed down. I couldn't experience most feelings any more, and felt incredibly anxious when being in contact with another human being.

Then there was the constantly dry mouth and excessive thirst. The rashes everywhere. The almost total loss of long-term memory. The weight gain. The blurred vision and the constant ringing in the ears. I was always tired – not just weary, but totally exhausted. And breathing was always erratic, and sometimes nearly impossible

The doctor eventually came up with the diagnosis that I was stressed.

Thu 12.02 pm

The 22nd of November was the day I met Lori. And Holly. And Kerry. And Maya.

My cyber marathon was a huge success.

This was in part down to my new, demographic, research-led approach to seduction. I'd identified phrases and questions that would lead to the maximum response from the target market in chatrooms, and weeded out the non-performers (including the old chestnuts such as, 'What do you look like?' and 'Are you rich?').

I also toyed with the idea of being truthful, but instantly rejected it.

Lori was going under the name Melba, and she wanted to know if I was a real lord. I confirmed that I was. She was from South Carolina, part Native American and an engineer.

She was somehow different. She asked questions instead of waiting for me to do the asking.

Her life was the same kind of soap opera existence as Jacqui's. In Lori's case, she had been left to bring up a baby single-handed after her husband beat her once too often, and she ended up in ER, while he ended up in jail.

She wanted to get away, maybe to Miami where her mother lived, but simply had no money. There was a sister nearby, but they hadn't spoken since the sister took a shot at her after a disagreement.

But the bit that really got my attention was her liking for older men.

'They're more mature,' she explained.

 # Fri 5.08 pm

I was in the bath, studying my rash. It seemed particularly red and itchy, which was most definitely not a good thing, since Kate was due to arrive in a little over two hours.

I hadn't heard from her for a couple of days, and half-presumed she'd got cold feet. That didn't stop me being more nervous than I could ever remember. I must've washed my body at least five times, probably in an attempt to make up for all the months of neglect.

An hour to go and I was pacing around the house, just wanting to get it over and done with. I'd arranged the lighting so that any room in the house where there was the potential for seeing me naked (and therefore my rash) was very dimly lit.

It occurred to me that I didn't really know this woman at all. I'd never met her, and now we were about to have sex – before introducing ourselves. Not surprisingly, this had never happened to me before.

 ## Fri 7.42 pm

Two and a half hours later I was experiencing a mixture of relief and frustration that she hadn't turned up. I'd just about worn out the carpet pacing up and down (well, I would've done, had it not been already completely threadbare) and it was good to be able to start winding down after all that tension.

I lay in bed and rang Kate's number. I just wanted to know why she changed her mind. No reply.

Then I heard a timid knock on the front door.

 ## Fri 8.12 pm

There were two things I noticed about Kate.

The first was that she looked better than her photo. She was medium height and slender with long, silky auburn hair. I liked her nose – it reminded me of Meg Ryan's. The awful Dame Edna glasses didn't do justice to her deep brown eyes, and she had a tight, disapproving mouth that made her look rather stern. Having her hair pulled back accentuated that look. Not what you'd call pretty, but, then again, neither was I.

The second thing was that she absolutely reeked of alcohol. But since we'd taken a vow of silence, I kept these thoughts to myself.

She tentatively stepped inside the house and put a finger to my lips. In the dim light I could see that she was wearing a simple, low-cut black dress, black stockings and stilettos.

I lifted the dress to check her underwear. These things are very important to me. Black and lacy matching bra and knickers. Excellent.

She then unbuttoned my jeans, while I stood there casually, as though this kind of thing happened on a daily basis.

We kissed, and the attempts to undress each other became increasingly frenzied. Her breasts were exactly as she'd described – firm and on the small side. I touched them, which got the foreplay over with.

I led her to the bedroom, making sure that she was on the side where my rash wasn't quite so bad, laid her on the bed and entered her.

About fifty seconds later, I was flat on my back, exhausted and spent. While we still weren't talking, the expression on her face said it all too clearly: 'Is that it?'

 Fri 8.39 pm

When we finally did get around to having a conversation, I learnt that she was twenty-four and gullible enough to believe my claims that the next time would be better.

We discussed how weird it was meeting people off the Internet. It transpired that she'd met a few men for coffee, but hadn't clicked with any of them.

She told me that the photo I'd sent her was almost enough to make her change her mind. It wasn't a flattering picture at all, but the only one I could find, since I'd avoided cameras for years, due to looking so ill. It was denial of the highest order – if I can't see photos of me looking ill, then I must look okay.

It was this kind of thinking that had me convinced there was nothing abnormal about almost total social withdrawal.

Eventually, the combination of alcohol, tiredness and almost a minute's wild sex was too much for Kate, and she fell asleep in my arms.

Her gorgeous, naked body was pressed against mine at 11.30 in the evening. And I could think of only one thing.

North American college girls would be logging on to the Internet right around now.

Fri 11.07 pm

Kate was a heavy sleeper, so I managed to get out of bed, switch the computer on and get into one of my ever-expanding list of favourite chatrooms without waking her.

The modem's shrieking sounded even louder than usual in the still night, and I wondered how anyone could possibly sleep through that. I had a contingency plan in case she awoke – a story about my lifelong struggle with insomnia.

Maya was the real reason. She was a girl I'd met during my marathon. She intrigued me because she was funny, confident and had such good taste that I didn't have to pretend to like things I hated.

She worked in a bookshop in Burlington, Vermont, where she specialised in finding obscure titles. Her proudest claim was that she'd successfully tracked down a book called *Raising Snails for Food*.

Her passion was acting, particularly Shakespeare. She was smart, she could spell and she was someone I could easily fall in love with. This meant that I had to worm my way out of some of the lies I'd told her when we met. I'm not even sure why I lied. I think I just got bored with the truth. It seemed so mundane.

Apparently I'd told her I was in publishing. I squirmed out of that by telling her I was a bit premature telling her about it, since I'd been negotiating to buy a small, local publisher, but the deal had fallen through.

I'd also claimed I was thirty-four. Although when I heard she was only twenty, I desperately wanted to revise it downwards. Still, she didn't seem to mind.

She was significantly more cultured than me. Every time she mentioned an obscure play (well, I'd never heard of *Juno and the Paycock*), I'd look it up on the Internet before giving her my considered opinion on it. On this occasion, however, I obviously wasn't concentrating because I said,

'*Oh yes, I remember Juno – Irish uprising, tragic heroine, etcetera... Isn't she pregnant? And unmarried?*'

She appeared confused and informed me that Juno wasn't pregnant, but her daughter Mary was.

It was the same with art.

Monet's paintings of Rouen cathedral were something else I'd never even heard of. Yet after looking through the right websites, I found plenty of intelligent things to say about them. Things I'd sprinkle into the conversation to show how clever I was.

I got the impression she didn't need such assistance.

Sat 7.25 am

While Maya was waiting for me in the chatroom, Kate was waiting for me in the bedroom.

She hadn't actually said anything, but I heard her coughing and making general 'I'm awake' type of noises. I called out to her, telling her to stay where she was and I'd bring her a nice cup of tea.

I put the kettle on and greeted Maya.

'Can't stay long,' I typed, 'but I just wanted to let you know I'm thinking of you.'

Then the strangest thing happened. I was totally overwhelmed by guilt for the way I was ignoring Kate, despite not knowing what, if anything, I felt for her – or what she felt about me.

I told Maya I had to go, but would talk to her later. Then, armed with a cup of tea, I went back into the bedroom.

Kate was still naked, and I climbed in beside her.

The thought crossed my mind that perhaps this was better than Internet life. A real, live person. One who was looking at me in an adoring way, despite having spent the night with me. One who I could sit and watch TV with (my ambitions were somewhat limited at this stage). And one who I wouldn't need to lie to about my age or appearance.

Wasn't a bird in the hand supposed to be better than two in the bush?

As part of my excessive guilt feeling, I confessed what I'd been doing. And then it all poured out. How the Internet had become my life, and the people seemed like real friends. I must've sounded maniacal.

She asked if I wanted to see her again.

 # Sat 3.42 pm

After Kate had gone, I waited a decent amount of time (about ten minutes), before taking up my customary position in front of the computer.

There were two e-mails waiting for me. One from Jacqui and one from Maya.

Jacqui's had a photo attached. It was her in a kilt. She looked nothing like the glamorous creature of previous photographs, but more like a pale, overweight woman with very bad hair. This was bigger than big hair, it was huge hair.

Judging by the kilt and the fact that she was posing by a plaque to 'The immortal memory of Sir William Wallace', I guessed she was in Scotland. This was confirmed by the mail, which read:

Hi...
You won't believe this. I'm in Bonnie Scotland! Och aye!
Sorry I haven't written, but I've been busy, busy, busy. The flight was great and the people here are great. The sites have taken my breath away and I managed to find out about the tribe my ancestors came from.Trevor, I have met a guy. He's Scotch and he's wonderful. You'd just adore him!
He wants to move over to the US just to be with me and Courtney! What do you think?
Jacqui

All I could think was that she'd written an entire e-mail without using the phrase '*per se*'.

 # Sat 4.12 pm

I was deeply depressed by Jacqui's mail. Never one to take rejection well, I was now being rejected by someone I'd never even met.

Maya's e-mail remained unopened. I couldn't bear the possibility of being rejected by her as well.

I decided to phone Kate and tell her all about it. She was becoming someone I could confide in about my Internet adventures without feeling embarrassed. We'd even talked about our own relationship, and decided that she'd come down again in a month or so, and stay for longer this time. That way, we'd know if it was going anywhere.

On the home front, a phone call from the people I had my mortgage with informed me that the arrears were simply too high and I would have to be out of the house within eight weeks. The situation was beyond repair.

I had to move out. Apparently, they'd written to inform me of this, but I hadn't opened the letter.

I had no home, no furniture and no assets. But I still had the Internet. Or so I thought.

Sat 9.39 pm

Kate also advised me to carry on talking to Maya, which I interpreted as being given permission for whatever might develop.

She also thought I should open Maya's e-mail because I couldn't possibly feel any lower than I already did.

So I read it. She was answering my latest round of questions. What was the most embarrassing CD in her collection? It was *The Sign* by *Ace of Base*. And the biggest fashion mistake in her wardrobe? Paisley print jeans.

In other words, a normal Maya e-mail. Which was a major relief.

She also told me she'd sent a tape that day and that I was to listen to it closely before making up my mind. Apparently, she thought I judged things before giving them a chance.

I decided to go to our chatroom to see if she was around, and went through the usual ritual of logging on. Only this time, something was terribly, terribly wrong. I was getting error messages.

In a blind panic, I ran to the phone to check if there was a problem with the server, but the phone wasn't working.

It slowly dawned on me that my worst nightmare had come true.

The non-payment of phone bills meant I had been cut off. Cut off from my Internet world.

I had never felt more helpless.

Sat 10.14 pm

The house was virtually bare. Since my focus had been entirely on the computer, I hadn't realised the combined effect of selling furniture and having goods repossessed.

The living room had a wooden chair and a lot of books. I had about 400 CDs and nothing to play them on.

And the computer. Not long ago, my lifeline to the world. Now a worthless grey box.

I sat on the chair, wondering what on earth I could do. It was only half an hour since I'd been online, but it felt like forever. I wondered how many e-mails had arrived, and whether Maya had found someone else in my absence.

I switched on the TV and watched infomercials for a while. Got bored, and went for a walk to the kitchen for comfort food. I found three potatoes and stood and watched as they boiled.

There was nothing in the fridge, so I had them on their own.

Five years before, I'd given up smoking. Just stopped. This felt similar. That same jittery feeling, where the slightest sound made me jump. I sat by the computer, running my fingers over the keys, eyes closed, imagining I was in the comfort of one of my chatrooms.

It was killing me.

I went to bed at around seven o'clock that night. And stayed there for four days.

Thu 6:02 pm

I got up only because Bernie, one of my few remaining friends, had dropped round, worried. He'd been trying to ring me, but got the disconnected tone.

I think he was shocked by my appearance. I was even more dirty and dishevelled than usual, and completely pale and drawn. I felt (and looked) exactly like I'd gone through a very tough drug withdrawal.

My speech was stuttering, and I made no sense at times. I felt disorientated, stuck somewhere between the real world and my safe little Internet world.

Bernie listened to my tale of woe, and asked for the phone bill. I told him to look through the big pile of brown envelopes on the floor, which he did.

The next day I heard quite possibly the most beautiful sound in the whole world. The phone rang.

Bernie had paid the bill and I was back.

 **Fri 1:52 pm**

The first person I chatted to wasn't Maya or Kate or Jacqui, but Lori (aka Melba), the South Carolina woman I'd spoken to briefly during my marathon.

She was clearly drunk.

'Come and sit on my knee, English guy,' she wrote, *'and share this bottle of bourbon with me. Not much left but it's yours.'*

So I replied with, *'English guy goes over to Melba and sits on her knee.'* It seemed churlish to tell her I didn't drink.

'English guy wants to know what Melba's wearing.'

'Just a flimsy old baby-doll nightie and nothing else.'

She then wanted to know where I'd been, so I told her all about my involuntary exile.

'Seems to me you got yourself kinda addicted.'

I denied it and then realised that was exactly what an addict would do. So I came clean.

'When we spoke last time, you wanted to see my pic. Still want it?' she asked.

'Very much – can you e-mail it to me?'

'Sure can. Wait there. Okay, sent it. Let me know what you think.'

I got her e-mail immediately, and the picture was a good one. Very good. I could see why she got the kind of male attention she seemingly hated. She was very striking-looking, big brown eyes, dimples and a wide smile. She looked a bit like a young Cher. Or a Cher of any age really. It all added up to yet another woman I was about to fall in love with.

She wanted a picture of me, so I promised I'd get some taken. I had a brainwave. If I got some black and white shots taken, I wouldn't look so pale and tired.

'*You still there, hon?*'

'*Sorry,*' I replied. '*Just taking a look at your pic. You are, if I may say, a very beautiful woman.*'

'*Why thank you. So what would you like to do to your Melba?*'

'*I'll tell you what I'd really like to do. Hear your voice. Can I call you?*'

'*Sure. Just give me a few minutes to get my shit together.*'

Fri 2:28 pm

'Hi, is that Lori?'

She giggled, the most delightful giggle.

'Well, I guess I know who this is.'

The giggling continued. As I'd suspected, she wasn't entirely sober.

'So, English guy, what do you want to know?'

'How about what you're wearing?'

'I just told you that in the chatroom – baby-doll nightie – remember?'

Oh, God. It was such a reflex question. A couple of weeks before, I'd rung Directory Enquiries because I'd mislaid Kate's number. After the woman gave it to me, I asked her what she was wearing. Really, I did it without thinking. As soon as I realised what I'd done, I slammed the phone down, and wouldn't answer it again that day, just in case she'd reported me to someone.

Meanwhile, I had to think of something a little more intelligent to ask Lori. So I asked about her horrible husband.

'He left after the beating,' she said, 'I haven't seen or heard from him since.'

'Why did you marry him in the first place?'

'I guess I just felt sorry for him. He would come into the store every day, bringing me flowers and telling me jokes. I never found him attractive, but he just wore me down.'

'What does he do for a living?'

'Nothin'. Well, he'll sometimes work for his uncle, painting houses.

Gets his weekly cheque off of the government, spends it all on booze and weed. I don't get a cent for my daughter. Matter of fact, he tells people she isn't his.'

'So is he good to her?'

'Hell, no... if she makes a noise when he's watching TV, he'll throw stuff at her. When she tried to stop him hitting me, he told her, "I brought you into this world and I can take you out."'

'Why did you stay with him?'

'Where else was I gonna go?'

'Your parents?'

'My ma thinks the sun shines out of his ass. All my fault, she says. Never did like me. Look, I gotta go. Talk to you tomorrow.'

I was left staring blankly at the receiver. Was it something I'd said?

 ## 9.02 am

In exchange for paying the phone bill, Bernie had insisted I see a psychologist, who might be able to get to the root of my problems.

After much phoning around, I managed to find one who did home visits. Her name was Shirley, and she specialised in phobias. I found this tremendously encouraging, since the worst aspect of my illness was agoraphobia, which meant going outside veered between uncomfortable and unbearable. She didn't sound fazed when I described my symptoms, and we made an appointment for the following Monday.

It all seemed so obvious, I wondered why I hadn't done it before.

At some level, of course, I knew I was simply ignoring my illness and choosing to focus instead on futile romantic involvements with girls in distant lands. By now, I was an old hand with them, so falling for Maya, who I would probably never meet, didn't faze me.

When I was at primary school, I fell hopelessly in love for the first time. I was eleven and thought Sue Lloyd was the most gorgeous creature who ever lived. I worshipped her – even struck up a contrived friendship with her brother so I could see the inside of her house.

Her family moved to Canada and my heart was well and truly broken. The fact that she'd never shown the slightest interest in me didn't seem to be a factor. I vowed that when I was old enough, I'd go and visit her.

When I reached sixteen, I joined the Civil Service in London, working in Somerset House, doing things with people's wills. I'm not entirely sure what I did, but I know I did it with a minimum of efficiency and enthusiasm.

One summer I decided to go and see Sue, even if it meant throwing away a not-very-promising career, so I worked out my notice, bought a return ticket to Toronto and dreamt of a tear-filled romantic reunion.

The reality of what happened couldn't be more depressing. The look of utter indifference on her face when she opened the door will never leave me. Nor will the look of benign amusement on her boyfriend's face.

I spent the entire ten days with Sue's brother, earning enough money to live on for the next couple of weeks. When I left, she wasn't even around to say goodbye.

Sat 12:15 pm

Maya and I met in our chatroom every night as soon as she got home from work.

I sent her flowers. Not real flowers, but cyberflowers. Pictures of flowers. Which is not quite the same thing.

We had 'our song' – *Whole of the Moon* by the *Waterboys*. This was chosen because we had decided that if ever we felt alone, we should look at the moon and know the other was also looking at it.

In conversations with my few remaining friends, I would refer to 'Maya and I', as in, 'Maya and I don't think that Douglas Coupland's latest book is very good.'

It must've been hugely annoying for them, but for me it felt like being in love with a real person.

We even played games. Chatroom games. My favourite was when she played the part of an unfaithful wife and I was her soldier husband, serving in Germany.

We'd stage massive arguments about her right to have fun while I was stationed overseas, and my right to have a faithful wife. The story got more and more elaborate, as it transpired she was sleeping with my brother.

Everyone in the room would take sides, and talk about it long after we'd (officially) left.

I really wanted to talk to her on the phone, but was too nervous. She felt the same way, so we decided to leave it for a while.

We sent each other little gifts. For my birthday she wrote me a fairy tale, about Princess Maya and Prince Trevor. It followed the traditional fairy-tale route, and I was beaming with joy when I read that we finally met at the end.

Never once did I ask her what she was wearing, or ask what she looked like.

 # Mon 11.30 am

A knock on the door dragged me away from the computer.

I opened it and found myself face to face with a severe and prim-looking woman in her late fifties or early sixties.

Her face didn't look as though it was used to smiling. She had close-cropped silver hair and wore no make-up. The only decoration she allowed herself was a pair of dangly shell earrings that almost touched her shoulders.

'Trevor? I'm Shirley Lockett. Psychologist. We made an appointment,' she said, in what was presumably meant to be a soothing, understanding voice. The earrings twitched and wobbled as she spoke.

I invited her in, petrified that she would notice the collection of female underwear spread over the sofa. I sat her by the window so it would be out of her view.

After giving her a bit of background and admitting that I spent much of my time on the Internet, she asked me if I had many friends I could talk to about my problems.

I thought for a while before replying.

'Yeah, a few I suppose. Let's see, there's Melba, Lady Gwinnivear, Princess Aurora, LadyDay. Well, LadyDay22, actually…there's a LadyDay26, but I'm not really friends with her…'

Shirley leaned forward, pursing her lips and inhaling deeply through her nose before asking if these friends were people I'd found on the computer.

I admitted that they were.

She nodded slowly, her face still contorted in an expression that I'm sure was meant to convey a deep intelligence. Unfortunately, it just looked as though she had a nasty taste in her mouth and was quietly biding her time before she could spit it out.

'I haven't been able to go out for about three years now. I get these panic attacks. I don't know why exactly.'

Shirley suddenly became frighteningly intense. Her nostrils flared and her lips became more pursed than ever, as she whispered maniacally:

'Yes, you do! We all have these answers inside us, Trevor. And I can help you find them. But first, tell me what was going on in your life when these problems started.'

'Nothing, really. I had a good job, my marriage was going really well – and then it slowly happened. I started getting panicky when I tried to leave the house. Then I lost my job.'

'And how did that make you feel?'

'Crushed. Destroyed. Humiliated. That sort of thing.'

She leaned forward, nodding her head, which made the earrings swing violently backwards and forwards. Thinking that this was her way of encouraging me to continue, I carried on talking.

'Then things took a turn for the worse. My wife left me.'

'I see,' she said, nodding wisely, 'and how did that make you feel?'

'I wanted to kill people.'

'Anyone in particular?'

'No, just people.'

'I see.'

'Will you be able to help me?' I asked, trying to keep the desperation out of my voice.

She lifted her right hand and moved her index and middle fingers to mimic the actions of tiny steps on the palm of her other hand.

'Baby steps, Trevor. That's what we must take. A little at a time. Here's how we'll start. No computer until after six tonight. Can you do that for me?'

I said that it would be no problem, and we made another appointment for the following week.

Mon 12.30 pm

After watching Shirley disappear down the path, I went straight to the computer, where there was a very interesting e-mail from Lori waiting for me. She told me that she'd bought a Polaroid camera, and my present was going to be some pictures of her.

I was to choose the poses.

I could choose anything I liked, she explained, because she'd arranged for a friend to take the photos.

I don't like to think of myself as too predictable, but what would you do? I requested nude shots, with as much detail as she 'felt comfortable with'.

Her only condition was that I should also get a Polaroid and take a picture of my penis for her.

I didn't have a problem with that, apart from wondering where the money would come from to buy the camera. In the end, I decided to sell some CDs, even though it meant getting about a quarter of what I paid for them.

She rang to say that her photo shoot was complete. I asked her to describe what I'd be getting, and she just said that I would be very happy indeed. Her friend had used up the whole film, which meant ten pictures. And now she wanted me to take my pictures. Right there and then. While we were talking.

I got the camera out and held it in my left hand. The phone was jammed between my right shoulder and head. My right hand was holding what Jacqui once referred to as my 'proud manhood'.

Taking a photograph like this is nowhere near as easy as it sounds. The first two attempts led to close-ups of the carpet. The next two were blurred, but made me happy because the angle made my 'manhood' look much bigger than it was.

At one stage I overbalanced while looking for the perfect shot, and ended up in an undignified sprawl on the floor, trousers around my ankles as the camera and phone flew across the room.

I was giving Lori a running commentary of all this. She was looking forward to seeing the pictures. And if she liked what she saw, she said she was just going to have to come over to New Zealand and find out if it felt as good as it looked.

Sun 10.10 am

Kate came back for another weekend, but it wasn't a success.

I think the fact that she was real worked against her. The Internet women had no flaws because I refused to consider the possibility that they had any. I'm sure it worked both ways – they would have seen me as perfect because that was what we all wanted to believe. It was a completely artificial environment.

And I loved it.

 # Mon 10.05 am

It was now three weeks before I had to move out of the house, and I hadn't done anything about finding somewhere else to live. I was so lost in the world of chatrooms and e-mails that it was now the outside world that didn't seem real. I literally had to force myself to look at the 'houses for rent' column in the paper. Since I was limited by my agoraphobia, I had to find a place nearby.

A familiar sight in chatrooms was a message from Lord Brett Sinclair saying, 'Back in ten minutes. Off to look at a house.' On reflection, this was something that would have merited more time spent on it. But it just didn't seem as important as chatting to my ever-increasing collection of women.

I found a really ghastly flat literally round the corner from where I was living. It had no redeeming features whatsoever – cramped rooms with low ceilings, the worst elements of 1960s architecture, a kitchen the size of a small closet, and a garden that resembled a swamp.

I took it.

The first thing I did was arrange for a new phone line to be installed so that I could get on the Internet as soon as I moved in. I decided to use some of the money from the house sale to upgrade my computer and also get some furniture.

I booked the removal people for early morning so as to cause minimum disruption to my chatroom routine.

Dave Roberts

 # Tue 9.28 am

The following day, as I was half-heartedly packing my few remaining possessions, the postman arrived with three letters bearing stamps from distant lands.

Two were from America, the other from Canada.

Holly had sent me a photo of herself in a bikini. She was a wholesome-looking blonde in her early twenties, who taught at Sunday school. We spent quite a bit of time talking in the chatroom. She had a boyfriend – in fact, she was getting married in just under a month – but romance seemed to be lacking. He apparently preferred playing paintball to being with her.

Kerry the Canadian had sent me a pair of her white silk panties (bringing my collection to eight) and a photo. She was in her last year of college and wanted to be an opera singer. A voluptuous woman, she reminded me of every opera singer stereotype you could think of. I'd told her about the pictures I'd sent Lori and she wanted me to take some just for her.

Amy, a recent addition to my cyberharem, had also sent me a pair of panties (bringing my collection to nine). Hers were covered in little flowers. I'd already seen her photo and liked what I saw. She worked as a secretary in local government, but had hopes of becoming a lawyer. And despite being twenty-four, she was still a virgin.

By now I'd spoken to all three on the phone. These were the type of calls that would normally have cost me $3.99 a minute. What should have worried me, but didn't, was that I was enjoying phone sex more than real sex.

And, of course, neither compared to cybersex.

 # Fri 10.30 am

The knock on the door woke me up and I ran to open it, hoping it was yet another package containing female undergarments.

It wasn't. It was Shirley the psychologist who must have mentally filed away the information that I had greeted her wearing a Pikachu T-shirt, which I'd bought online as part of a set of seven, the idea being that you could wear a different Pokemon every day of the week.

She got straight down to business, reminding me (using her fingers on her palm) that we needed to take baby steps in order to achieve our goals. She then moved on to the next stage of my treatment.

I had to shut my eyes and visualise a time I was relaxed. When I managed to conjure up such a memory, she got me to describe what I was seeing.

I vaguely recall mumbling something about walking along a beach, hand in hand with the woman I loved, my faithful golden retriever trailing us. A gentle breeze was blowing and the sun was setting in the evening sky.

It was only later I realised that this scenario was part of my cyberseduction routine (I tended to incorporate the name of whoever I was chatting to into the story) and hadn't actually happened in real life.

In hindsight, I can see why this strategy was staggeringly ineffective. It didn't really do much good in this instance either

After describing the scene to Shirley, everything was a blank until I heard her saying my name over and over again.

When I opened my eyes, she was gazing at me intently.

I must admit, I did feel quite relaxed. That feeling lasted for all of a minute, when she said she wanted me to go outside and take the feeling with me. I was to walk as far as I could and think of nothing but the scenario I had described.

I was petrified, but willing to give it a go.

It started well. I must have got 100 yards before I felt the first stirrings of anxiety. Around 20 yards further on, I started to feel light-headed and convinced I was going to faint. My heart rate felt as though it had doubled.

Suddenly, all thoughts of moonlit beaches had disappeared to be replaced by feelings of sheer panic.

I ran home as fast as I could.

Shirley told me, in her most sincere and reassuring voice, that I had done very well indeed.

Dave Roberts

Fri 11.52 pm

I realised things had got out of hand when the phone rang and a North American voice said, 'Hi, it's me.'

Well, as far as I was concerned, it could've been one of a dozen women. But I couldn't let her know in case it was someone I really liked. So I tried fishing for clues.

'Oh hi, how are you? Have you finished for the day?'

This was meant to elicit information about work/school to help me narrow it down, but she just said how busy she'd been. I was really panicking by now and was sure I was about to get found out. I tried another tack.

'I'm not sure I'm getting all your e-mails. Can you remember what the last one was about?'

'Ummm...no. Sorry.'

Then I had a burst of inspiration.

'Look, this is a really bad line. I can hardly hear you. How about if I call you back? You'll have to give me your number again...I can't find my address book.'

She gave me her number. I flicked through my address book until I found it.

'Okay, Lori,' I said as calmly as I could manage, 'I'll ring you right back.'

 ## Sun 10.21 am

Maya and I were now writing each other incredibly long letters once or twice a day. We swapped vital information, such as songs we really hated and words we found annoying.

I had to invent a semblance of a life because I couldn't see how anyone would be interested in someone who spent all day on a computer. So I peppered my e-mails with lies like, *'Have to go now – people are arriving for the fireworks party'*, or *'Looking forward to later – we're having a video evening'*.

At first our correspondence was the typed equivalent of a first date – the finding out about each other process. Now, they were getting increasingly intimate.

One day, she had an experience that she described as the strangest of her life. She'd stopped off at a second-hand record shop on the way home from work, and a man had started talking to her. They had an interesting conversation, but all Maya could think of was, 'Trevor looks exactly like this man'.

I took this as absolute proof we were meant for each other.

A friend of hers came up with the theory that the reason we felt we'd known each other for hundreds and thousands of years was because we had.

Apparently, we are all made up of atoms, each vibrating at a certain frequency. And when two people resonate to the same frequency, things like the record shop episode are bound to happen.

This theory appealed to my romantic side, so I took it as fact. Strange things were happening, though, which pointed towards some kind of connection.

I was falling deeper and deeper for someone I knew everything about, apart from what she looked like or sounded like.

 # Mon 9.47 am

I took the proud manhood photographs to the post office to send them off to Lori. Four of them had passed my quality control test; the rest, including close-ups of the carpet, had been destroyed.

It was while I was in the queue to pay for the card I'd chosen that I realised what I was doing. Sending a picture of my penis to a complete stranger. What if someone opened it by mistake? Or if it ended up plastered all over the Internet?

What if I got so overcome by nerves when I got to the counter that I dropped all the Polaroids and everyone could see what I was sending? What would I do?

I'd just want to run out of the door, back to the safety of my own little world, but then again, leaving pictures of your penis on the post office floor could have humiliating consequences.

These thoughts made queuing for a stamp one of the most stressful activities I'd had to face in many years. But as it turned out, I needn't have worried.

It all went smoothly. I paid for the card, wrote Lori a short note, put the Polaroids in the envelope and sent it on its way.

While I was out, I popped into the chemist for another Polaroid film.

 # Wed 11.14 am

Hannah was a Kiwi I met in the Chat Cabin, my favourite chatroom. I'd known her for a few months, and was anxious to find out how her cyber romance had worked out.

Her cyberlover was flying out from England to meet her, and both were expecting great things.

As soon as we started talking, I realised things hadn't worked out. Apparently, it started well, despite the fact he'd sent a photo that was at least fifteen years out of date – which made him at least fifteen years older than he'd originally claimed.

She was prepared to overlook this, since they clearly had something that went a lot deeper than the way they looked.

They met at the airport and went straight to her place, where they spent two days in bed, just enjoying being together after years of craving each other.

He'd helped her through a really tough divorce by being online during the long nights when she was first alone. She grew to rely on him for emotional support, and he was happy to help.

It seemed a pretty good basis for a relationship, and at first he seemed really happy to be with her.

Then, after two days, it became clear that he was feeling a little restless. He decided to spend a week camping in the South Island and 'getting his head together'. He was unable to articulate what was wrong, and instead just stopped talking.

That was the last time she saw him. I couldn't help but wonder if Maya and I would be the same way when we finally met.

Thu 9.15 am

Lori's pictures to me arrived the day before mine reached her.

They were everything I'd hoped for. There she was, in all her naked glory in a variety of poses, some of which left absolutely nothing to the imagination.

I thought that whoever took these photos had to be a very, very trusted friend.

My favourite was one where she was sitting up in bed, playing with her tits, which had fallen from her bra. It was far from the most explicit, but I found it the most erotic.

I also liked one where she was wearing a short nightie – quite possibly the baby-doll one she'd mentioned previously.

I went into the bedroom, spread the pictures on the bed and locked the door.

Fri 2.36 pm

I found some buyers for the house about five minutes after it went on the market.

They looked a nice enough family, and I even tore myself away from the computer long enough to answer a few questions about the location of schools and shops.

The price they offered was way more than I expected, and I agreed to it before they had time to change their minds. If they'd been aware that the building society would have been happy with a lot less, they might not have been so generous.

It was going to be tough leaving, though. A lot had happened in that house, and not all the memories were bad. While the marriage may have been pretty awful for the last couple of years, it was good before that.

I had only a week before I had to leave. A week in which I'd spend 130 hours online and twenty hours packing.

 **Fri 8.10 pm**

I was so eager to talk to Maya that I got into the chatroom almost an hour before we were due to meet.

Our romance was well known amongst the regulars, and several asked me how it was going. I admitted that things were getting quite serious and that we were officially a couple. At least, as far as I was concerned.

When Maya got there, she seemed a bit subdued, and when asked what was wrong said that she didn't want to tell me because I'd hate her.

I tried to change the subject, but my heart wasn't in it. I had to know, even if it was the unimaginable – that she'd found someone else.

She made me promise that I'd give her a chance to explain. I reluctantly agreed, even though I was shaking. What she told me was this...

She'd been for a drink with some of her colleagues after work, and at the bar she met up with someone she'd had a one-night stand with the previous year. They got talking, had a few drinks and he invited her back to his apartment for a nightcap. When they got there, he made his move and started kissing her. She went along with it and they ended up in bed.

She was feeling so guilty that she burst into tears afterwards and told him to get her a taxi. When she got home, she tried to write me an e-mail explaining what had just happened and how it didn't mean anything, but the words wouldn't come out right.

Now she wanted to know how I felt. I couldn't think straight. Suddenly, the room felt terribly claustrophobic. I had to get out.

It was a clear night and I found myself walking rapidly up the road, away from the house, away from the computer, away from Maya.

I looked at the moon and was overwhelmed by sadness. I just stood there until the anxiety took over and drove me back indoors.

Chapter 3

 Fri 10.07 am

Moving house was nowhere near as traumatic as I thought it would be. My strategy of moving the computer first paid off. It meant that while the removal men were doing all the hard work, I was in my new bedroom and online.

I was sitting on the floor, typing away. Apart from the computer, the flat was completely empty.

Now while this may paint a picture of abject poverty, the reverse was actually true. For once in my life I actually had money in the bank. My share of the house sale was enough to pay rent for a year, get some decent furniture and pay Bernie back for the phone bill.

I also vowed to do something about my health, and one of my online friends had suggested I see a naturopath, since conventional medicine didn't seem to have any answers.

I rang the naturopath, Peter Collins, and arranged for him to come and see me the following week.

Maya was constantly on my mind. I hated the thought of her with someone else, and wondered if things could ever be the same between us. I hadn't written to her since hearing about her one-night stand, but was planning a romantic reunion.

Just then, one of the removal men put his head around the door and held up a shopping bag full of women's panties.

'Where do you want me to put these, mate?' he said.

Sat 12.45 pm

The only person I ever met on the Internet who embraced cyberlife with the same passion that I did lived two streets away from my new flat.

Her name was Leanne, aka GingerKiss.

Of the forty-two men who had flown or driven to Wellington to see her, she had slept with twenty-eight, planned to move in with seventeen, become engaged to eight and ended up with none.

She was always ringing me in a panicked tone, demanding I come round and rescue her from her latest boyfriend/fiancé.

On the rare occasions I was feeling well enough to get round to her house, I met a wide spectrum of men. My favourite was Alastair. He was a slight, bald chap with round glasses and a love of DIY that bordered on obsession. He and Leanne were having a small party to celebrate their moving in together. We were discussing the house, which had met with his approval for the seemingly bizarre reason that it was built on a bed of solid concrete.

'You can't beat being on a slab,' he announced with such feeling that I'd swear I saw a tear forming in his eye. It was one of the great conversation killers of all time.

Another fiancé was called Martin. He was perfect. A psychologist in the corporate sector, he was starting to get a good reputation for his painting, and had had several exhibitions. Not only that, but back in the 1970s he'd played guitar in one of my favourite punk bands – *Eddie and the Hot Rods*.

Unfortunately, he wasn't quite what he seemed.

The psychologist in the corporate sector thing turned out to be a vague plan he had for the future. He didn't actually have a job 'at this point in time'. The art exhibitions were technically true – he held them in his garage. I went online to check out *Eddie and the Hot Rods*, and, as expected, no one of his name had ever had anything to do with the band.

A man I never got to meet was the one known only as 'the one who kept doing the stary face thing after he spoke'. He lasted only one date, and she never even planned to share a house with him. They met at a Turkish place, and his entire conversation was about how Auckland had much better weather than Wellington.

At the end of a boring evening, she asked how they were going to pay. He reluctantly said that he didn't mind, before staring at her with a slightly worried expression.

The next day she got an e-mail from him saying that he'd had a great time but was disappointed he had to pay. She wrote back, pointing out that she had offered to split the bill.

His reply was to suggest that she pay $40 as her share.

She sent him a cheque, he sent her a receipt and they never saw each other again.

 Mon 8.10 pm

Lori rang in a complete panic.

'Honey, I've got a confession to make.'

Oh, God. What now? First Maya, now Lori. My Internet world was rapidly falling apart.

'Well, you know I told you about my husband?'

'Yeees...'

'And I told you how we were no longer living together?'

'Yeeeees...'

'Well, I was kinda stretching the truth a little.'

'What do you mean? Are you still married?'

'Well, see, the thing is, he kinda refused to move out. I'm not sleeping with him or anything, but he still lives in the same house.'

'But why didn't you tell me?'

'I guess I didn't think you'd understand.'

'What's to understand? The guy beats you, abuses you, treats you like rubbish, spends all your money and you let him stay with you.'

'It's not like that. Oh, Trevor, you don't know him – he's crazy. I can't just make him leave.'

'What about the police? Can't they help?'

'They keep arresting him, they keep letting him go. At least they confiscated his gun after he last tried to shoot me. But like he says, he'll just get another one.'

'Geez, Lori. Well, I suppose it can't get any worse.'

'Yes, it can. I haven't told you the real bad news yet.'

'Which is what?'

'Those pics you sent of your cock. He found them.'

 # Wed 9.35 am

Peter Collins, the naturopath, was whippet thin with lots of pent-up energy. He got straight down to business.

He listened as I detailed my medical history and, unlike the doctor, didn't look with disbelief when I went through my symptoms.

He asked questions that, at first, didn't make a lot of sense. Like how many metal fillings I had in my mouth. And which foods I ate regularly.

He told me I had mercury poisoning. It seems that the mercury in my fillings was slowly leaking and getting into my bloodstream.

My expression must've told him that I didn't believe him because he opened his bag and got out a small tube of mercury. He then put a paperback book on the table and told me to pick it up. I did. He then held the tube next to my bicep and told me to pick up the book again. I couldn't. My arm felt too weak.

He had me convinced.

The bad news was that I had to have all my fillings removed. All seventeen. Without anaesthetic, which I was allergic to.

Yet I couldn't wait to get started. The chance to get my health back was the one thing I wanted most in life.

 # Thu 10.15 pm

There was an angry American man on the phone, but I couldn't quite understand what he was saying. It sounded like:

'Youfuckwidmywifeyougonnagettabulletindabrainasshole.'

'Pardon me?' I enquired.

'Youfuckinheardmeasshole.'

'Look, I could make out something about a bullet in the brain, but you're really going to have to speak a little more slowly.'

'You…know…izzackly…what…I'm…talkin'…about. Asshole.'

'Oh, you'd be Lori's husband?'

'Fuckin'-ay I am. And she's married to me. So stop fuckin' sendin' them fuckin' pictures. I'm gonna fuckin' kill you, asshole.'

He sounded as though he meant it. He continued his rant.

'I would of gone over there and killed you soon as I found out, but I'm givin' you a chance. Leave my wife alone and I let you live.'

'Would have.'

'Whassat?'

'Would have. You said "would of" gone over there. But that's incorrect grammar. You should say "would have".'

'Fuck you, asshole. I'm gonna kill you. I got the bullet right here and it's got your name on it.'

'Look, Arlen, you haven't been living as man and wife with Lori for months. You sleep on the sofa and she can't wait for you to leave. She doesn't want you around. Got that?'

'Well, that ain't right. We live together, we sleep together – not that it's any of your damn business – hell, we even got a daughter together. So next time you wanna break up somebody's marriage, you find someone else. You got that, asshole?'

'You mean you never split up? And you're staying married?'

'Damn right!' he said, ending the conversation. 'And she won't be callin' your ass again. I've made damn shure that.'

 ## Fri 08.30 am

That morning, I got a letter in the mail that I had written around three years previously.

Dear Mr Niblock

To recognise the value of your business to the bank, you've been pre-approved for a Premier Card with a $5000 credit limit. Many of our customers have found that a Premier Card simplifies their everyday banking.

To receive your pre-approved Premier Card, complete the attached form and return it in the reply paid envelope.
Yours sincerely

Dave Ferris
Marketing Manager

Dave Ferris. That bastard. First he fires me and withholds my hard-earned money, now he wants me to have a credit card.

Of course, he wouldn't have known he'd sent me this letter. My unusually healthy bank balance had meant that I was automatically sent it. Nonetheless, it planted the seed of an idea that would not only help me get my own back, but also make my Internet life even more enjoyable.

Thu 9.35 pm

Holly, the wholesomely pretty Sunday school teacher, was in our chatroom.

We had a bit of a role-playing thing going on. She was Lady Ayla, a beautiful yet lonely young woman, living in the shadows of a misty village in the Middle Ages. She always concealed her features with a large cloak. It was good for her enigmatic image.

I, of course, was Lord Brett, the incredibly good-looking and sophisticated gentleman who was going to rescue her from her mundane existence.

We spent a lot of time taking long walks in the moonlight, hand in hand. The moonlit walk is something of an Internet tradition.

At the start of every chatroom romance, one person will ask the other 'So, what do you like to do?' and the reply will be any combination of the following (although the first two are virtually mandatory): moonlit walks on the beach, hanging out, partying, listening to music, rollerblading.

So Lady Ayla and I took cyberwalks along moonlit beaches. Lay down on the cybersand and watched the cyberwaves crash into the cybershore.

We cyberkissed in the shadows. It was a perfect, undemanding romance.

The only cloud on the horizon was that Lord Brett had a rival for the affections of Lady Ayla.

A man known simply as Roger.

Roger was a sad, middle-aged loser, whose real life was so unsatisfactory that he'd taken refuge in chatrooms, preying on innocent young women to fuel his sordid desires.

In other words, he was exactly the same as me.

And this chatroom wasn't big enough for the both of us.

 Fri 5.33 pm

I wrote Maya a short e-mail.

Hi Monkey [That was my pet name for her – neither of us could quite remember how it came about.]
Let's start again. Let's meet as strangers in the chatroom and fall in love. The past never happened.
T

I then sat back and waited for the reply. Every minute that went by seemed an eternity. Perhaps I'd overreacted and she'd had enough. Or maybe she'd lost interest in the Internet (and me).

I got up in the middle of the night to check my e-mail. Nothing.

By morning, I'd been up five times.

As a sign of my fragile emotional state, I even tried hypnotising the computer. 'An e-mail from Maya will arrive, an e-mail from Maya will arrive,' I repeated in the soothing monotone of a TV hypnotist as I stared at the screen.

I toyed with the idea of ringing her, but thought that would only make matters worse. After the longest thirty-six hours of my life, I finally got the e-mail I'd been hoping for. It simply read:

Oh monkey,
I'll be waiting for you. Come soon.
M

Sun 2.03 pm

After Arlen discovered the pictures of my intimate parts I really, truly thought that Lori would be lying in a hospital somewhere, so the relief when she rang was unimaginable. I hadn't dared ring her in case it antagonised her husband even further.

She said it'd be safe to talk because The Asshole was flat out in bed, drunk.

She got the bad news out of the way first. Not only had he found the photos, but he'd read my e-mails to her. He'd gone berserk, threatening all sorts of retribution against me.

He was going to hack into my computer and destroy everything. He was also going to hack into my bank and wipe out all my money. She kept giggling as she told me this because his computer skills were apparently limited to turning one on and off.

She genuinely didn't seem scared of him. Unlike me.

I told her about his call to me, and the death threats. Now, I'm not a brave man, and even the cushion of 8000 miles didn't ease the anxiety. She assured me that there was no way he'd carry this out. He had no money and had never been outside South Carolina.

Despite this, I was still worried.

That afternoon the seed of a plan had been planted in some dark corner of my brain. I don't know whether it was motivated by sex, compassion, love or simply the need to make grand, sweeping gestures, but I had decided to buy Lori an air ticket to come and visit me.

The rationalisation went something like this: she's stuck with a violent husband, wants to leave him but has no money and nowhere to go, so why not use my new-found wealth to get her over and see how it all works out?

I did feel a genuine fondness for her. The qualities I admire most are determination and courage, and she had plenty of both.

There was enough room in my horrible little flat for her and Cheyenne. It could be the start of a new life for us all.

Lori thought it was a great idea.

Tue 9.13 am

The song *You're Gorgeous* was one of my favourite songs of the nineties and its heart-on-the-sleeve romanticism appealed to me.

As I was listening to the words, I had an idea. The CD would be an incredibly romantic thing to give to a girl, with a note reading something like 'I heard this and thought of you'.

I bought twelve copies online, then sat down to write twelve identical notes, before dispatching twelve packages to all corners of the globe.

Thu 11.08 am

With my internet life and real life set to collide, it was time to embark upon another drive to recover my health. First, I made an appointment with Mr Duthie, the dentist just down the road. Then I started looking for other things that might help

The experiment with Shirley the psychologist hadn't been a success, but some online research had opened up one or two promising new avenues.

There was a word for this. Cyberchondria.

It means diagnosing yourself with all sorts of diseases and illnesses via information gleaned from the Internet, and finding cures.

Sometimes, these could verge on the bizarre.

I was particularly intrigued by ear candles.

The testimonials were most impressive. People whose lives had been blighted by anxiety had found the answer by sticking lighted candles in their ears, which had removed the toxic debris by literally sucking it out.

It had to be worth a try, so I ordered a couple of packets.

Thu 11.08 pm

Maya and I met up in the chatroom for the first time since her confession.

We acted as though we'd only just met, and were both treading very warily.

We discussed our favourite *Jerry Springer* episodes. Hers was *We Live in a Car*, in which a young couple lived in a 1987 Subaru wagon.

The woman's family objected on the not-unreasonable grounds that her partner was a loser and couldn't provide her with the life she deserved.

Naturally, it ended up with everyone hitting each other.

My vote went to *600-Pound Angry Mom*, in which a mother, who weighed 600 pounds, was angry with pretty much everything. Her no-good kids were no help at all, and she had to do everything herself. Including getting dressed.

Naturally, it ended up with everyone hitting each other.

This small talk was necessary. We had a long way to go before we could trust each other again. I had been badly hurt by what I saw as her cheating, and she had problems with a man who ran away and cut off all contact rather than face difficulties.

We both realised that the fresh start, which I'd mentioned in my brief e-mail, was worth a try.

'Hi,' I typed, *'I'm Trevor.'*

'My name's Maya. Pleased to meet you.'

'So, Maya, where you from?'

'Burlington, Vermont. You?'

'I'm from the UK, but living in New Zealand. What do you like to do?'

'Oh, I like long moonlit walks on the beach. You?'

'I like long moonlit walks on the beach.'

'Well, since we both like long moonlit walks on the beach, I think you should call me. It sounds like we have a lot in common.'

'You seriously want me to call you?'

Panic coursed through my veins. This was the girl I was in love with, and we'd never actually spoken. Now, a few months after meeting online, we were finally going to hear each other's voices.

It was agreed that I'd call her the next day, after I got home from the dentist.

I started to write a script of questions and witty off-the-cuff observations. Spontaneity had a habit of deserting me when I needed it most.

Fri 8.13 am

Sleep is surprisingly difficult when you know you have to get up at 8.15 and have six fillings removed without anaesthetic. Especially when the same thing is going to happen on the next three Monday mornings.

I had to force myself out of bed, force myself through the door, and force myself to walk the 100 yards to the dentist in plenty of time for my 8.45 appointment.

As I stood outside his door, my courage deserted me and I started running home as fast as I could. Unfortunately, I ran straight into the dentist, who was on his way to work. Mumbling something about having a morning jog, I walked back with him and sat in the waiting-room as he prepared his various instruments of pain.

Going through to the surgery was like walking along death row. Being a small, suburban practice, modern technology was not in evidence. The chair looked straight out of the 1940s, as did the equipment. The dentist, who was elderly and had a worrying shake in his right hand, probably came from an even earlier era.

I'd read about pain-free fillings done by laser, and was hoping against hope that he'd produce one of these devices at the last moment.

Instead, he examined my teeth through the thickest lenses I'd ever seen on a pair of glasses, and then attached a huge needle to his drill.

'Is this going to hurt?' I asked.

'Yes,' he replied.

He was right. It was the most painful experience of my life.

When I got home an hour and a half later, my mouth was in agony. I couldn't eat, I couldn't speak. But at least I could log on to the Internet.

 # Fri 10.24 am

Later that morning, I got a bullet in the mail.

It was sent anonymously, but considering the envelope was postmarked South Carolina, I had a pretty shrewd idea who was responsible.

But if I was shaken by that, what happened next left me a

nervous wreck. That night someone tried to set the flat on fire. I smelt burning, so went out the back, where I found some firewood had been soaked in petrol, placed against the side of the house and lit.

Luckily, it hadn't caught properly, but I was shaken enough to call the police.

They arrived surprisingly quickly and started asking me questions. A dog-handler tried to pick up the scent, while another two quizzed me.

Had I lived here long? No, only a few weeks.

Did I have any idea who'd want to do this? Well, maybe.

What did I mean? Well, I've just had my life threatened by a jealous husband. The female officer eyed me with scepticism. I could see her point.

The latest happenings had left me even paler and tireder than ever. I wasn't an attractive sight.

She asked for the name and address of the jealous husband.

'I'm not sure,' I explained. 'He lives in South Carolina.'

'And do you have any reason to believe that he's in the vicinity at present?'

'Well, no. As far as I know, he's still in South Carolina. But he did send me a bullet this morning.'

She sighed and put down her notepad.

'May I see it, sir?'

I handed it to her. She took a cursory look and placed it in a plastic bag.

'So, you can't think of anyone who might want to start this fire?'

I decided not to let my paranoia go any further. There's a time and a place for conspiracy theories involving South Carolina rednecks and Nazi sympathisers in Wellington, and this wasn't one of them.

'No,' I replied.

Fri 6.33 pm

If the thought that someone wanted to set my flat on fire made me a nervous wreck, the thought of ringing Maya made me absolutely petrified.

I gave myself deadlines and watched helplessly as they passed.

I contemplated inventing a sore throat, or another ailment that would get me out of talking to her.

In the end, I forced myself just to sit down and do it.

She sounded like Phoebe out of *Friends*. God knows what I sounded like. Squeaky, probably.

I was also trying much too hard. I used up a full page of pre-prepared comments/ad libs within the first two minutes, and had run out of things to say after about three.

With e-mails and chatroom conversations, you have the ability to edit, rethink and delete if necessary. There's no such luxury when you're talking. You get only one chance to say the right thing.

As a consequence, I restricted myself to giggling wildly every time she said anything remotely funny and answering questions in as few syllables as possible.

We somehow managed to talk for an hour, although it was the longest hour I've ever experienced, including the one recently spent in the dentist's chair.

I think we were both happy to put the conversation out of its misery, and get back to an area where we both felt more comfortable.

So we went straight to our favourite chatroom, where we talked non-stop until sunrise.

Sat 5.43 am

Just before I went to bed, I checked my e-mail. There were twenty-four of them, of which twenty-two were from Lori's crazed husband, Arlen.

The vast majority of these were incoherent, but I think I got the message.

He was going to kill me. Other threats included:

1.   Hacking into my bank's computer.
2.   Sending my penis Polaroids to a customs agent he knew.
3.   (and this was possibly the weakest) Telling Lori I was a fag.

He often talked about his 'people'.

'*I got people in the airlines business,*' he'd claim. '*I got people in Customs.*' And so on. This drunken, workshy little man apparently had people throughout the world.

'*Watchyer back, asshole. I got people in your country,*' was another notable example. He claimed that he'd been talking to a New Zealander in a chatroom, who was so incensed about what I'd done that they'd offered to put a bullet through my brain.

Although I was taking this fairly lightly, I always had the thought in the back of my mind that he might actually do something. I knew he belonged to a white supremacist organisation, and I wondered whether they'd have contacts locally.

Having someone try to burn the flat down was what the Americans would classify as 'a wake-up call'.

Besides, Lori had sent a photo of him and he looked mean. Scrawny, ugly, psychotic-looking, he wore a T-shirt proclaiming *The South Will Rise Again,* and a tattoo announcing his allegiance to White Power.

Apparently, no one took him seriously.

Except me.

Sat 11.24 am

My ear candles arrived after a night of fitful sleep, notable for a recurring nightmare about being chased by a mean, ugly, psychotic-looking individual, who was wearing a shirt proclaiming *The South Will Rise Again,* and a tattoo announcing his allegiance to White Power.

I decided there was no time like the present for putting the candles to use and getting rid of the toxins that were making me ill.

Following the instructions, I lay on my side and lit one of the candles. Then, having placed a mirror by the sofa, I slowly eased it into my ear.

It had to go in as far as the line, which meant the candle was almost an inch inside my ear canal.

The sensation was actually quite pleasant, once you got used to the idea of lying on your side with a lit candle sticking out of your head. My only worry was that someone I knew would come round and look through the window to see if I was in. However, given that my life was lived almost exclusively online, there wasn't much danger of that.

After a while I could feel the heat inside my sinuses and whatever other passages there are in my head.

It was incredibly relaxing.

After the first candle had burnt down to the recommended level, I did the other ear.

I then opened the burnt candles to study all the toxic debris I'd been harbouring all these years.

There was nothing there.

Thu 10.31 pm

Holly, the Sunday school teacher, was in our chatroom and she was talking to Roger, my bitter rival.

I knew he'd talked to her on the phone quite a lot recently, and made several hints about having an affair. He was married, but after thirty years, boredom had set in.

He was a musician and had written several songs for her, which he'd play over the phone. Being a Sunday school teacher, she really wasn't interested in an affair, but I could tell she was flattered.

'He probably sings that song to all the girls and tells them it was written especially for them,' I said, sulkily.

'Oh, don't be silly, Trevor. Anyway, guess what I got this morning? That wonderful CD you sent. I've played it so many times already. It's so awesome, and I love that it reminds you of me. Do you really think I'm gorgeous?'

'The most gorgeous girl on the Internet.'

'Awww. I'm not, but I'm glad you think so.'

Roger had gone awfully quiet at this stage, but suddenly came to life. *'You got that right, Lord Brett. She's one beautiful woman.'*

It was time to up the ante. Crush this Roger once and for all.

'My lady, there is something I must know.'

'Yes, my dear?'

'Over the months I have fallen deeper and deeper in love with you.

Will you cybermarry me?'

'*Why, Brett. Of course I will.*'

I still had some unfinished business. A question for my rival that was designed to cause maximum offence.

'*Roger, will you be the best man?*'

 ## Fri 9.20 am

I rang the police to see if anything was happening with my complaint about death threats, and they told me there was nothing they could do.

I don't know what I was expecting really. Maybe to hear that they'd locked the madman up and thrown away the key. Or put him to work on a chain gang. Or sent a posse of FBI agents to surround his house and shout through a megaphone, 'Come out with your hands above your head! We know you're in there!'

But no, it seems that barely coherent death threats via the Internet came down low on the priority list of international crimefighters.

I was informed that Arlen wouldn't be able to come to NZ without them knowing, and that they'd 'interview' him at the airport. This was slightly reassuring, and gave me comfort every time I heard noises in the night.

Meanwhile, the flow of e-mails from Arlen was showing no signs of abating. He'd come up with a few new threats, but generally stuck with the tried-and-tested 'bullet through the brain' one. That was his favourite. If he'd known that his wife and I were planning to live together, he definitely wouldn't be happy.

 ## Sun 11.25 am

Lori was making plans to move out.

The idea was that she'd escape to her mother's house in Florida in the early morning, while Arlen was still passed out drunk.

She was going to stay there for a month, tying up some loose ends, before flying out to be with me. She'd already started packing, under the pretence of going away for the weekend.

Her mother was coming to pick her up, after Lori managed to convince her that she needed to get away.

I knew Arlen wasn't going to take this lightly. He was extremely possessive, insisting on knowing what she was doing and who she was seeing every time she left the house.

He even told Lori that they'd be together through all of eternity and that no one would ever come between them.

The escape had been planned with military precision.

She knew exactly what she was going to take. Her personal belongings were few. He'd searched her room, looking for letters and photographs from me, and when he found them, he burnt them all. Including letters and mementos from her childhood.

He knew all her hiding places because he was so used to trying to find money for alcohol and drugs.

But Lori had a fitting revenge in mind. She was going to do two things she thought would upset him more than losing her and his daughter.

She was going to take the big screen TV and pour all his beer down the sink.

 ## Mon 1.28 pm

Maya and I had managed to put the phone call debacle behind us and were back to being chatroom lovers.

It was hard to see how we were ever going to meet. She'd decided to go to London for a couple of years, just to get away from her comfortable Vermont environment. I had no such desire. I was very happy in mine.

Once, when I was feeling pretty optimistic about recovering from my illness, I mentioned that I might go and see her. We even talked about maybe living together in London. I've always wanted to go back some time, and maybe the time was right.

On her birthday – her twenty-first birthday – I sent a bouquet of her favourite flowers. A real bouquet, not a cyber bouquet. They were waiting on her doorstep when she arrived home from work.

It was the first time in my life I'd sent a woman flowers, and she was delighted. Even took a picture of them.

At the same time, she got one of the security guards at work to take her photo. Which meant I'd finally get to see what she looked like.

In my mind, she was a perky, slim blonde, who was beautiful in a general perky, slim blonde kind of way. I knew she was attractive because customers were always hitting on her. Besides, she'd described herself as 'cute'.

I picked out an old photo of me that best hid my blemishes. It was a black and white one, and in it I looked vaguely intelligent. In fact, I thought I resembled Alan Rickman. No one else thought this, incidentally.

Maya was sending her photo by mail. I was sending mine by e-mail. So she'd see my face long before I saw hers.

I clicked send and waited to find out if she would still be in love with me when she saw what I looked like.

Mon 11.03 pm

Now that living with Lori was about to become a reality, there were one or two lies I was regretting.

There was nothing I could do about my alleged seven-inch penis other than to try one of those enlargement devices I received several e-mails about on a daily basis.

But there was something I could do about the size of the rest of my body. A quick survey amongst the citizens of my chatroom came up with the conclusion that the Atkins Diet was perfect for losing weight quickly. And I had to lose thirty-five pounds so I could reach the 200 pounds I'd told Lori I weighed.

The Atkins Diet sounded bizarre. Apparently, if I ate nothing but protein, the weight would fall off me.

So I planned out the day's dishes. Eggs and bacon for breakfast, a huge steak and eggs for lunch, with a dinner comprising cheese, lamb and bacon. All washed down with a glass of milk.

I couldn't wait to get started.

 **Tue 11.03 pm**

I was cybermarried at eleven o'clock tonight, while my bride was cybermarried at seven o'clock this morning.

The time difference meant that most of the guests were American.

We'd been unable to find someone to conduct the ceremony, mainly because I forgot I was supposed to organise it. Luckily, at the last minute, a chatroom regular who went by the name of Macduff stepped in.

Not surprisingly, Roger had declined my invitation to be best man, but at least he showed up. Holly had spoken to him and he was devastated. Apparently, the dividing line between reality and cyberlife had become as blurred for him as it was for me.

Macduff was clearly revelling in his role.

'We are gathered here, in this chatroom, to witness the wedding of two people we know and love so much. Sweet Holly, who has broken so many hearts, mine included, has chosen to pledge her troth to that rogue, Sinclair. I now call upon Sinclair to make his vows.'

This was surreal. Around eighteen people, sitting at their computers, pretending to be at a pretend wedding.

'Ahem.' I began, *'I have known the divine Holly for nearly two months and have cherished the time we've spent together. I know that had we met in real life instead of here, we would make each other extraordinarily happy. My heart belongs to you and only you, darling Holly. And as I place this cyber ring on your finger, I want you to know that you're gorgeous and I'd do anything for you.'*

Okay, so I ran out of inspiration towards the end and had to resort to using stolen song lyrics, but overall I was pretty pleased.

It was her turn.

'M'lord, you have shown me that true love overcomes all boundaries, like where in the world we live and our differing ages. You are the wind beneath my wings.'

Noooo, not that song. Pleeease.

Macduff took over and brought a hurried end to the ceremony.

'I now pronounce you cyberhusband and cyberwife. Ladies and

gentlemen, let the festivities begin for Lord and Lady Sinclair.'

The bastard. He'd done that deliberately. If any of the girls I was involved with in other chatrooms saw that there was a Lady Sinclair, my cyberlife wouldn't be worth living.

 ## Wed 10.47 am

By this stage, I no longer bothered reading Arlen's threatening e-mails. There was no point. I already knew what they were going to say.

The only novelty was wondering how many variations he would be able to come up with for the spelling of 'vengeance'. But even that paled after a while. In fact, the whole Internet novelty thing was beginning to wear off.

Whereas at the start a chance cybersexual encounter would turn into a marathon performance of superstud proportions, it was now over in minutes. The entire act had been condensed into a perfunctory 'So I throw you down on the bed, whip your knickers off and...oh God, I've come'.

This may have been a lot more true to life, but was unlikely to find its way into any textbooks under the heading of *What Women Want*.

The problem was that I was getting much too much of a good thing. I was online for sixteen to eighteen hours a day, and had long since lost count of my cyberlovers.

Obviously, a break away from the computer was out of the question, but I made a decision. I was going to concentrate on my main cyber romances, and turn at least one of them into a real-life fairy story.

I was planning to marry Lori, Maya or Holly.

 ## Wed 1.42 pm

Lori loomed as the most likely candidate for my second wife by virtue of the fact she was coming to live with me.

Her husband had become increasingly paranoid, for good reason. He now drank at home all day instead of drinking at the bar all day.

He would just sit and watch her, saying nothing. There was no way of knowing what thoughts, if any, were running through his mind.

The night of the planned escape had arrived and I couldn't have been more nervous. I felt powerless. I was powerless.

Lori seemed remarkably composed. She'd managed to pack everything that she and Cheyenne were likely to need, and even her ever-watchful psychotic husband didn't seem to bother her unduly.

The plan was for us to meet in our chatroom while he drank himself into a stupor. Then, when he had passed out, she was going to call her mother, who was staying in a nearby motel with her latest boyfriend.

My job was to reassure her.

Of course, she ended up having to reassure me, telling me that she was going to be fine and that nothing would go wrong. She would call me once she got to Florida. In the meantime, I wasn't to worry. Then the words I'd both looked forward to and dreaded appeared on the screen.

'*Honey, he's passed out. I'm gonna call my mum. Wish me luck. Love you.*'

And with that, she was gone.

 ## Wed 9.22 pm

As I was daydreaming about a real-life wedding to Lori, I found myself having a cyber honeymoon with Holly.

Since money is no object in Cyberworld, I decided that we would spend a week in a small Norwegian village.

I started typing.

'*I pick you up in my private jet. I am dressed in a black tuxedo, white shirt, black bow tie, black shoes.*'

She replied with, '*I climb into your jet, taking care not to trip on my white flowing gown. I kiss you tenderly, feeling your hard body pressed against mine.*'

Oh, God. Hard body. Did I really tell her that? It was my turn.

'*We sit in the cockpit, looking at the night sky. Before we know it, the plane has landed and we have taken a limo to the small hotel. The snow is falling, but our room has a log fire.*'

In the old days I would have stretched the scenario out for ages, including the most painstaking, irrelevant details. Now, I just wanted to get on with it, even if it meant cramming eighteen hours of activity into a few short sentences.

'Wow, you're moving kind of fast, Lord Brett.'

'It's only because you look so ravishing tonight that I can't wait to make love to you for the first time. I pull you towards me and kiss you.'

'I stroke your face gently, looking into your deep brown eyes, seeing the candlelight reflected.'

'I tear your dress off and lay you across the four-poster bed.'

'No, not yet.'

'Oh, okay. I kiss you again, my tongue sliding inside your mouth, as I reach for your breast.'

'NO! Not yet.'

'Right. So...we kiss?'

'Yes, we kiss. Gently. I feel your heart beating quickly. It is beating with love for me. We gaze at each other in the gentle candlelight as a string quartet plays downstairs.'

'Oh, right. I see what you're getting at. So...we sit down at the window and watch the snow gently falling? That kind of thing?'

'You got it, my darling cyberhusband.'

Suddenly, I realised that my knowledge of women was even less than I'd previously feared.

Wed 11.03 pm

My cyber honeymoon was rudely interrupted by the phone ringing. But the annoyance was soon replaced by joy.

It was Lori.

She was calling from the motel where her mother was staying. The escape had largely gone to plan, although they'd taken the precaution of getting the police along to make sure Arlen didn't try anything stupid.

As it happened, it was a good move. As the car was being loaded, he had stumbled outside and, when he realised what was happening, completely flipped out.

He tried to drag Lori back inside, telling her that she belonged to him and if she left him, he'd come after her and kill her.

Apparently, the cops just looked on while this was taking place, and Lori's mother's boyfriend had to come to the rescue.

This did nothing to soothe Arlen's anger, and he told them all he was going to get his gun so he could sort this out once and for all.

Fortunately, by the time he got back outside, the car had been packed and they were already driving away.

The last thing Lori heard from Arlen was a phrase I'd read and heard many times since making his acquaintance.

'Vengeance will be mine!' he shouted, as the car disappeared into the distance.

 # Wed 11.58 pm

After that brief but exciting intermission, it was back to the honemoon.

I'd learnt my lesson, or so I thought.

'I'm back, darling. Just had to take an urgent call. It was my Geneva office. I told them they were interrupting my honeymoon, but they insisted it was a matter of life and death.'

I think that was the point when I could no longer distinguish between fantasy and reality. Why couldn't I just tell her I'd been on the phone? Why did I have to incorporate it into the story?

'That's all right, darling. I guess I'll just have to get used to it, being married to such an important and powerful man.'

Christ! I wasn't the only one with reality problems.

'But I've sorted the problem out. Now, take a look out of the window. See those skaters on the frozen pond?'

'Yes, I do, darling.'

'Can you read what they've carved out in the ice?'

'I can't quite make it out. What does it say? Your eyes are better than mine.'

'I believe it says "Thank you, Lady Sinclair, for making me the happiest man on earth".'

My God, I was pleased with that one. And so was she, apparently.

'I rather think it is time we went to bed, my lord.'

 **Thu 10.28 pm**

Lori had arrived in Florida. And waiting for her was a letter from her ex-husband. His strategy had changed. He'd decided to woo her back with poetry.

She read out what he'd written.

My darling rose who is my life
You and Cheyenne make me complete
You are the only one for me
I bow at your feet.

Surprisingly, this failed to generate the kind of response he'd anticipated. In fact, she was laughing so much, it took her at least five minutes to finish.

There was more. He'd sent her a soft toy. A small, pink cuddly bear. Unfortunately for him, she recognised it as one she'd bought for Cheyenne last Easter.

The win-back-Lori campaign also included phone calls. Lots of them. In one day, he called her thirty times. He was going to change, he vowed. He never realised how much he loved her until she'd gone.

Yet as soon as she told him she had no intention of coming back, his mood changed. He told her he had people in Florida who would make her sorry. He was also going to talk to his lawyer and get the TV returned, plus custody of Cheyenne.

But if she just came back, he would make her happy.

To prove his love for her, he'd already quit boozing. Although since he was slurring these words, they didn't have much credibility.

His final gesture was the most magnanimous of all.

As long as she moved back in, broke off all contact with me and started behaving like a real wife, he would forget all about taking vengeance on her.

Chapter 4

 ## Fri 10.05 pm

I was loving the Atkins Diet.

For years I'd been sensible about how much meat I ate, and now I could have unlimited amounts.

I was starting to have snacks on an hourly basis.

Sausages and lamb chops. Followed an hour later by eggs and ham. Then it was time for lunch.

It was costing a fortune. But since it was a way of improving my health, I felt it was worth it.

I was also starting to buy cheese in huge blocks and sour cream in massive tubs.

I don't think I'd eaten so much in my life.

 ## Sat 11.12 am

I was still hopelessly in love with Maya.

In fact, I was more in love than ever since she'd told me how handsome I looked in the photo.

I hadn't seen hers yet, but was expecting it shortly and the anticipation was wonderful because I knew it wasn't going to affect the way I felt about her.

I've heard cyberpeople claim that they don't care what their cyberlover looks like, but always dismissed it as nothing more than a reasonably effective line. Yet I really didn't care.

We'd created a little fantasy world, imagining that we were living together. We liked to talk about doing simple things together: sitting on the sofa, watching TV, taking moonlit walks along the beach.

It seemed to both of us that it was only a matter of time before this came true. She told me that she considered herself 'taken'. I told her the same thing, conveniently forgetting the likes of Lori and Holly.

Neither of us mentioned having another attempt at a phone conversation for fear of spoiling the entire fantasy.

When her photo finally arrived, I sat out on the porch and stared at it for about half an hour.

Her hair was dark brown, not blonde. And she had that expression you see in so many pictures. The one that says 'Don't point that camera at me'.

In my eyes she was every bit as beautiful as I'd expected.

My Kiwi cyberfriend Hannah had recently (and inexplicably) become involved with an asparagus farmer from Vancouver. He set new standards in dullness. I know because she forwarded some of his e-mails.

He had suggested that he sell up and move over to New Zealand, where they could set up an asparagus farm together.

To demonstrate how idyllic this would be, he'd used computer trickery to create a picture of him and her standing in a field (presumably one full of asparagus).

I thought that was the cheesiest thing I'd ever seen.

Until I did the same thing, to produce a picture of Maya and me standing in a garden, my arm around her, both of us with camera-shy expressions on our faces.

 Sat 10.03 pm

'You like Bridget Jones?' I typed with enthusiasm. *'Me too. I've read the books hundreds of times.'*

I was chatting with Bridget McJones. You can't always tell much about a person from the nickname they use, but in this case I had correctly deduced that she was (a) a fan of Bridget and (b) Scottish.

'That's great,' she replied. *'Which book did you like best?'*

The question threw me. Not because I couldn't decide on my favourite, but because I'd been lying about liking *Bridget Jones* in order to ingratiate myself.

Predictably, it wasn't long before I was found out.

'*I think I preferred the one where she was single and had to go on a diet. That was really funny.*'

'*Memo to self: must stop chatting with Lord Brett as he's not always truthful.*'

'*You mean you worked out that I've never actually read any of the* Bridget Jones *books?*'

'*v good.*'

Other things I've claimed to be interested in while pursuing cybersex include:

1. The music of *N'Sync*.
2. Cats.
3. The theory that everything happens for a reason
4. American football.
5. Poetry.
6. Gardening.

 Mon 10.03 am

It was the day of my first weigh-in.

I felt confident as I stepped up to the new electronic scales that I'd bought from eBay especially to measure my progress.

I knew they were the most advanced scales on the market because they had been developed using cutting-edge NASA technology.

When I started the diet I was 235 pounds.

Today, after a week of nothing but protein, I had dropped down to an incredible 112 pounds. A loss of 123 pounds in just seven days.

Either this was truly a miracle diet, or the scales weren't quite as reliable as I'd been led to believe.

 # Mon 11.14 pm

Arlen's poems were arriving at Lori's temporary house with alarming frequency. She was being bombarded by bad poetry.

The latest, I was flattered to hear, featured a cameo appearance by me.

If that asshole hadn't met you on the Internet
Our love would have bloomed like a rose in spring
I would have followed you anywhere
I still would give you anything

He was also regularly filling up the tape on the answering machine.

The messages would start out tender and romantic, like: 'Honey, it's your husband, Arlen. I just wanted to say that I love you and Cheyenne, and that the house is empty without you here. You are both my life. Please come back.'

By the end of the tape, a less conciliatory tone had emerged.

'Lori, where the fuck are you? This is your husband and you belong to me, dammit, so get yer ass back this instant or I'll fuckin' come and teach you a goddamn lesson.'

When the phone next rang, she answered it. It was Arlen, of course, drunk and barely coherent. He wanted to talk to Cheyenne and tell her how much he missed her.

Lori handed the phone over to her daughter and went to the kitchen to make a coffee. When she got back, she asked Cheyenne what her daddy had to say for himself.

'He said that we was going home soon and be a real family again. And he was going to buy me anything I wanted.'

'Is that right?'

'But then he got real mad when I told him we was going to live with Trevor in New Zealand. He said to stay right here because he was coming to get us.'

Mon 10.23 am

With Lori and Cheyenne moving to be with me, I realised that I needed to find a source of income. And as if that wasn't going to be hard enough, it also had to be one that didn't involve leaving the house.

An ad in the paper seemed to offer the perfect solution.

'Want to work from home and make big $$$$$?' it asked.

I nodded in the affirmative.

'Training provided. For free video, call 0800 29073.'

This sounded like the answer to my prayers. When you're stuck in the house all day, employment options are strictly limited. The only other thing I had followed up had been selling double glazing over the phone, but the commission was lousy and I suspected I wouldn't have done a very good job.

I rang the number and asked for my free video.

 # Sat 10.23 pm

By the time I arrived in the chatroom, my cyberwife was talking to Roger, my former cyber rival, and she was clearly uncomfortable.

He'd been interrogating her over the cyber honeymoon, asking for all the sordid details. He claimed that his interest was fatherly, and he just wanted to make sure she didn't get hurt.

But that didn't really explain the outburst of bitterness she'd had to sit through, when he told her that she'd ruined his life by making a very bad choice. Couldn't she see how wrong I was for her, and how right he was?

She tried explaining that she was getting married for real that weekend, but that only angered him more. It must have seemed that he was one of the few men to miss out on marrying her.

He reminded her that he was prepared to leave his wife for her, which was bizarre. They'd spoken on the phone a few times, but she'd never given him any encouragement.

But what really frightened Holly was how much Roger seemed to know about her life. He somehow knew lots about her fiancé. He also knew things like the name of one of her bridesmaids, the church where the wedding was taking place and where they were going for their honeymoon.

Holly was positive she hadn't told Roger any of these things.

She had the feeling that something very, very bad was about to happen.

Mon 11.03 pm

Christmas is a terrible time for the Internet addict.

The chatrooms are deserted, like cyber ghost towns. Only the truly, irredeemably, chronically lonely are left. Those with even a semblance of a life find reason to spend at least one day a year offline.

I found myself chatting with an old man from Edmonton in Canada, whose wife had left him and whose children had flown the nest. He wanted to reminisce about Christmases past, and since I had nothing else to do, I was a willing listener.

Christmas had always been the happiest time for him, which is why it was now the saddest. It was only a year ago, when the entire family were together and now here he was, on his own, with only me for company.

He told me about how he first met his wife. She was working for a delivery company and an important package he was expecting hadn't arrived.

He was furious and called the company, demanding an explanation. She took the call, calmed him down and went off to find the package, which she then hand-delivered to him.

He fell for her instantly, asked her out and six months later they were walking down the aisle.

Their marriage had been wonderful. This year would've been their fortieth anniversary, and in all that time they'd never spent a day apart. They'd had two smart and beautiful daughters, one of whom was now working in Saudi Arabia and the other in Berlin.

I had to know what could have destroyed such an idyllic marriage, the kind of marriage I'd always dreamed of having. So I asked him, as gently as I could. His answer was the last thing I wanted to hear.

'What happened? Oh, she met some guy on the Internet.'

Tue 8.18 am

That Christmas was like all my Christmases coming at once.

I'd never been more popular with women in my life. There were Christmas cards from dozens of them, including three different Karens, a couple of Sarahs and even an Olga.

It's conceivable that these weren't all spontaneous outpourings of affection. A series of blatant hints and, in a couple of pathetic cases, grovelling requests were behind my apparent popularity.

My usual technique was to say something like, '*I sent your Xmas card today – have you sent mine yet?*'

One of the few unsolicited cards had come from Kate, the only woman I'd been brave enough to meet in real life. Her card was nice and chatty, telling me about what she'd been up to, and finishing with:

> *By the way, did you ever find out who tried to burn your house down? That must have been really scary!*
> *Love from Kate*
> *xxxxxxxxx*

Something about that was troubling me, but I couldn't work out what it was. Until I suddenly realised – the arson attempt had happened after I'd broken off contact with her.

There was no way I could've told her about it.

 # Tue 12.18 pm

Another gift I got for Christmas was, according to the letter accompanying my free video, a solid financial future.

I immediately put the tape into the video machine, then sat back and watched as three grinning Americans stood proudly outside huge houses with huge cars, looking very happy with themselves.

A man's voice explained why. It said, in a confident, authoritative tone: 'What do Ted DiMarco, Alan Mitchell and Luanne Irving have in common? They're regular folks, just like you and I – the difference is that they have become multimillionaires using a secret they now want to share with you.

'You see, Ted, Alan and Luanne are all part of the worldwide Herbal Solutions family. Before they joined us they had careers, but weren't satisfied with where they were headed. So they decided to take charge of their financial destiny.'

A glossy-haired presenter then appeared with a range of herbal products. He explained: 'We have products for you to share with everyone – your friends, your neighbours, your co-workers. Everything from certified weight-reduction programs to all-natural relaxation aides. To find out more about a career with the Herbal Solutions family, call this toll-free number now. You won't regret it.'

The presenter then winked, before adding: 'Just ask Ted, Alan and Luanne.'

In life, as on the Internet, you tend to believe what you want to believe. Which is why I firmly believed that Herbal Solutions would be the answer to all my financial problems.

I picked up the phone to make the call that would undoubtedly change not just my life, but Lori and Cheyenne's as well.

 **Wed 2.01 pm**

Lori and Cheyenne were on the run.

They'd left Lori's mother's house after hearing that Arlen was coming to get his daughter. I don't think it was the possibility of violence that scared Lori – more his threat to fight for custody of Cheyenne.

However unlikely it was that he could win, it was still a risk she didn't want to take. His parents were pillar of the community types, who would impress any court, let alone one in the same county.

She was staying with a friend in Austin, Texas, until her flight on Friday.

By now I was really looking forward to her arrrival. We'd talked about it endlessly. We both knew of a couple in our chatroom who had met up and got married. They each had their own computer room in the basement, and at night they'd go in there and chat. They didn't talk to each other until it was time for bed. We weren't going to be like that.

Lori was going to get a job, maybe four nights a week, and I was going to take care of Cheyenne, as well as build up my Herbal Solutions empire (which I hadn't yet told her about – I wanted it to be a surprise). She wanted me to call a few strip clubs to see if they had any vacancies for dancers.

'Strip clubs? But I thought you were an engineer?'

'Honey, I am an engineer. But I danced my way through college. And we're gonna need some bucks in a hurry. Don't worry. I know what I'm doing.'

Well, I knew she wasn't shy about her body. And with good reason. But I hadn't really seen the next stage of my life consisting of living with a stripper, looking after her daughter while she worked, and selling herbal products. When would I find the time to go on the Internet?

 Wed 9.55 pm

When I saw I had an e-mail from Holly, I presumed it was to tell me about how well the honeymoon went.

I couldn't have been more wrong.

Trevor:

I don't know what to say... Well, goodbye is a good start.

This will be my last e-mail to you, I guess. Luke received an e-mail from 'a friend' telling him I've been a bad wife by cheating on him with you and talking about hooking up in real life. This 'friend' somehow got a hold of some of the e-mails we wrote to each other and sent them also. Luke is completely angry at me and doesn't want to be with me anymore. I've ruined my life, I guess... no house of our own... no kids... I don't know what I'll do. I guess just go on as if I'm fine when really there is no meaning to my life as my husband hates me. I am so sad. I will miss our talks but my marriage has to come before you. I doubt there is anything to save as he has already said no house and no kids. Maybe he at least will not leave me.

Holly

I knew straight away that the 'friend' was Roger. He worked with computers and had once boasted how easy it was to hack into web-based e-mail accounts. But how could he hate Holly this much? He'd never even met her, and she'd always made it clear that friendship was all she was interested in.

Yet here he was, destroying her life.

I felt weighed down with guilt. This harmless flirtation had somehow turned into a real-life tragedy. I briefly thought about ringing Luke and explaining everything, but decided that would do more harm than good.

The best plan was to leave them both alone and hope that time would start to heal the wounds.

What bothered me most was that I couldn't decide who was really to blame for the break-up of Holly's marriage. Was it Roger? Or was it me?

Fri 10.45 am

I decided to throw myself into my work.

One of the conditions of joining the Herbal Solutions family was that you had to have enough stock to meet the inevitable demand.

This meant spending a large chunk of my fast-dwindling fortune, but the brochures from head office assured me that there was no limit to the success I could have simply by working hard.

In the section entitled *How much money can I make from Herbal Solutions?* the answer was beautifully simple.

It said, *How much money do you want to make?*

These were my kind of people. I was convinced that the twenty-eight boxes of various products would be snapped up in next to no time.

Thu 8.22 pm

I picked up the phone and dialled a once-familiar number.

Kate didn't sound that happy to hear from me. Nor did she sound surprised when I asked her if she'd tried to burn my flat down with me inside.

'What, you think just because you treated me like shit and dumped me with no explanation that I'd try and kill you?'

'Well, yes, I was rather thinking along those lines.'

'Trevor, you flatter yourself. You don't think I'm proud of what we did, do you?'

Then, I don't know what came over me. Probably the memory of a fumbling encounter between two incompatible but desperate people filtered through rose-coloured glasses.

'I don't suppose you fancy coming down for the weekend?'

When someone puts the phone down on you, there's no way of telling if they're replacing it gently or slamming it down.

Chapter 5

 ## Mon 6.16 pm

My work strategy was to combine looking for Herbal Solutions sales opportunities with my all-day chatroom visits.

It wasn't long before an ideal opportunity presented itself.

I had met a Canadian student calling himself Neutrino Boy, who was complaining of the stress he was going through with his upcoming exams. Apparently his chatroom commitments – *'so many friends, so little time'* – had left him too tired to study.

I seized the opportunity. Grabbing a brochure, I asked him if he'd considered taking a dietary supplement. I then informed him that I happened to represent a company who made a perfect product for him.

'It's called Relaxo, and its active ingredients include kava kava and echinacea, grown in the unpolluted Inuit Islands.'

I then sat back, awaiting his order.

What I didn't expect was him to point out that the Inuit Islands were a frozen tundra, making it impossible to grow herbs there.

I promised to look into it.

 ## Thu 10.52 pm

Arlen sounded less than happy to hear my voice, which made me wonder why he'd called me.

It didn't take long for him to get to the point.

After a brief barrage of threats and insults, he informed me that Lori had come to her senses and had moved back in with him. He said she was cooking him dinner and had asked him to tell me to leave her alone because she loved her husband.

He added that his daughter Cheyenne was so happy to be home that she'd made him a present and said how glad she was that they weren't going to live with that asshole in New Zealand.

I would probably have believed him had Lori not called me from the airport twenty minutes earlier, telling me that they were about to get on their flight to Auckland via Los Angeles.

 ## Sat 3.42 pm

At the back of my mind was a nagging doubt about whether Lori could possibly live up to the Lori I had created in my imagination.

I remembered thinking Jacqui was my ideal woman, despite a few conversations that should have raised red flags.

One example of this was the time she was telling me she'd just watched a DVD of *Hamlet*.

I asked her which version.

'The William Shakespeare one, silly,' she replied.

On another occasion, she was sharing her interest in philosophy.

'As Platon once said,' she explained, *'we are all one soul in two bodies. We spend our lives trying to find the other half of our soul.'*

I asked who Platon was.

'He was a Greek. It's where we get the word Platonic from.'

 ## Sun 3.42 pm

There was really only one slight cloud on the horizon as far as Lori was concerned.

I'd never quite got round to telling her about my illness. The most immediate problem this created was that she was due to arrive in Wellington in an hour, expecting me to meet her.

Even if I had been well enough to get to the airport, which was something I hadn't managed in ten years, there was also the problem of my car — the 1986 Toyota Corolla that had belonged to my ex-wife and that we used to drive to work in.

Many years before, she'd kindly given it to me on a kind of permanent loan basis. Since then, neglect had taken a brutal toll. It had long ceased to be legal and roadworthy.

Every time it rained, the engine wouldn't start. Even worse, the roof leaked, adding to the pool of water on the floor of the passenger's side. The pool was now about two inches deep and was home to a variety of pondlife, including clouds of really annoying white fly-type creatures, which I had to continually swipe away while driving.

There was also an impressive little sapling growing out from somewhere between the front tyre and the door.

I suspected if I'd turned up to meet Lori in this, going back to Arlen would become a very tempting prospect.

 # Tue 8.22 am

My strategy was to cook a 'Welcome to New Zealand' meal.

Unfortunately, it was raining, so I couldn't drive to the supermarket. This meant using the food I had, which was mince, a couple of chicken breasts, lamb chops, a steak and about two dozen eggs

This would be familiar to anyone who has ever attempted the Atkins Diet. However, I was fairly certain that neither Lori nor her daughter were on it.

I scoured the Internet for recipes that included these protein-packed ingredients, hoping to come up with something exotic, but eventually conceded defeat.

It seemed that after a twenty-hour flight, they would be sitting down to a meal of meat and eggs.

Meanwhile, there was the equally pressing problem of how to explain my non-appearance at the airport.

Wed 6.57 am

I decided that I owed it to Lori to at least try to meet her.

I rang for a taxi, even though the thought of going all the way to the airport filled me with sheer terror. Breaking open the box of Relaxo, I swallowed a couple of packets. Anything to calm me down.

I then closed my eyes and imagined myself walking along a beach, my faithful dog following me as the sun set slowly. It made no difference at all. I was almost paralysed by fear.

Then, as the taxi pulled up, I ran out, wild-eyed with arms waving, screaming something like, 'Come on! Let's do this!'

 # Wed 10.27 am

The taxi driver looked surprised to see me rushing towards him with a maniacal expression on my face.

He was equally surprised when I climbed in the back and asked him to take me to the airport. About a minute later, as we drove out of my comfort zone, I was pale, shaking and dripping with sweat. I asked him to turn around and take me home instead.

I couldn't go through with it. And I knew that the disappointment I felt would be nothing to what Lori would be feeling.

 # Wed 10.55 am

She rang from the airport half an hour later.

I apologised profusely, explaining that my car wouldn't start, and that if she got a taxi, I'd pay when they got here.

She put the phone down on me.

This was getting to be a regular occurrence in my life.

Wed 11.29 am

I watched the taxi pull up and rushed outside to meet my wife-to-be and stepdaughter-to-be.

Two things dampened my joy.

The first was seeing the taxi driver. It was the same one who had driven me around the block a short while ago.

'How much, mate?' I asked him, hoping, rather ambitiously, that he wouldn't remember me.

The look he gave me indicated that not only did he remember me, but also that he felt my mental stability was in question.

I paid him and included an excessive tip to stop him saying anything.

The other thing that I found a bit disconcerting was Lori's reaction to me. She didn't rush into my arms.

She didn't shriek with joy at seeing me.

And she didn't look at me with undisguised lust.

No, the first words to pass from her lips were, 'Are you going to stand there all day or are you going to get our damn luggage?'

And then, for the first time, she smiled.

 # Wed 12.17 pm

I was in love.

She was unquestionably even more beautiful in the flesh than she was in her photographs, which had failed to capture the fact that she was a three-dimensional, living, breathing human being.

Cheyenne was great too. The first thing she did was to shyly hand me an envelope, which I opened a little over-enthusiastically.

It was a painting of me. It was gorgeous, although not strictly accurate, since it was based on a misleading photo I'd sent, which had been taken during slimmer, healthier, younger times.

I immediately realised that Lori and Cheyenne, who had flown halfway round the world just to be with me, probably deserved to be welcomed with more than a plate of various meats.

I told them that if they were up to it, I'd like to take them to a local restaurant for their first evening.

I then turned to Lori.

'So, what do you want to do now?' I said, with what I felt was a suggestive smirk.

'Sleep,' she replied, without a hint of suggestiveness.

Wed 3.35 pm

While Lori and Cheyenne slept in the spare room, I logged on to the Internet.

My plan was to tell anyone who had the slightest interest that Lord Brett Sinclair was officially off the market.

Not only that, but he would be retiring from chatroom life.

Many of my romantic interests had either disappeared or got bored, so it was difficult finding anyone who cared.

Disappointingly, Kerry, the would-be opera singer, took the news with casual indifference.

Amy the secretary asked if she would be getting an invitation to the wedding.

And Maya, who was meant to be my soulmate, had disappeared off the face of the earth.

She was the one I was going to miss most, and I was depressed that she'd never even said goodbye.

Our last chatroom meeting was one of the best.

We came up with a new game, which we called chatroom bingo. The object of this was to ask complete strangers leading questions and earn points according to their replies.

My favourite one was asking their philosophy. Now absolutely everyone in a chatroom has a philosophy on life, and it's never an original one. That's why the answer, 'Live every day like it's your last' got the full ten points.

'Carpe diem' or 'Seize the day' was worth eight.

'Life is not a dress rehearsal' earned six points.

'Live life to the fullest' got four.

'Dance like no one's watching' was worth only two points, while there was just one point for 'Aim for the moon – if you miss, you'll be amongst the stars', as well as for anything else to do with aiming high or stars.

Maya won the game by fifty-three points to forty-one.

 ## Wed 3.52 pm

I was going to miss spending my days in chatrooms.

I'd met some wonderful people there. I'd also met some very strange ones.

This final session was typical. I met a man known simply as Screenwriter, and a woman called Madonna.

Screenwriter wanted to chat with me about his latest project.

He'd written a screenplay that, he assured me, would blow everything else out of the water.

I asked him what it was about. He told me it was the story of a veteran, hard-headed cop who disobeys orders and leads a rookie on a two-man vendetta against crime.

It sounded familiar. I was pretty sure I'd seen at least five films with the same plot in the past twelve months alone. I asked him if he'd managed to sell it yet.

He told me that three producers were bidding for it.

I hoped he was lying, but had a horrible feeling he wasn't.

A few hours later I found myself in deep conversation with Madonna. Yes, *that* Madonna. The singer/actress/children's book author and wearer of red cotton around her wrist. She insisted she was the real thing and, despite many attempts on my part to catch her out, stuck to her story.

The only slight doubt I had was that we were in a New Zealand rugby chatroom at the time.

 ## Wed 5.25 pm

I woke my house guests later that afternoon, with a cup of coffee in Lori's case and a mug of hot chocolate for her daughter. In one of our last phone calls before Lori left America, we'd decided that this was the best way to overcome jet lag.

I really wanted to tell her about my health problems and explain why they meant I couldn't live a normal life, but I was scared she'd get straight back on the plane. So I decided to bluff it out and hope that she wouldn't notice.

I was absolutely dreading the night out, but since the restaurant was literally less than 800 yards away, I felt I had a chance of keeping my anxiety under control.

Since it had become obvious that Relaxo was 100 per cent ineffective and that the Inuit Islanders had been wasting their time growing the ingredients, I swallowed a handful of another Herbal Solutions relaxation product called R&R.

Then it was time to get ready.

I gave a rare outing to my charcoal suit, Ralph Lauren shirt and dark blue tie, which I'd bought for meetings back in the days when I had meetings.

Cheyenne looked very smart in her designer jeans and pink sequinned top.

And as for Lori, she changed into a simple black dress with suede boots.

I doubted that any woman had ever looked better.

Wed 6.38 pm

The brief drive to the restaurant had me reaching previously unknown heights of anxiety.

Not only was I anxious about going out for a meal, but I was also petrified that Lori's boots would get soaked in the pond by her feet.

To make matters worse, I then conjured up a scenario in my head where she was screaming at the shock of the cold water, and her open mouth was seen by the white flies as an invitation to go exploring en masse.

I put my foot down and got there before any harm could be done.

If she'd noticed the pond and flies (and it was hard to imagine they'd escaped her attention), she had clearly decided they weren't worth mentioning.

I wasn't sure if this was a good thing or a bad thing.

 # Wed 6.45 pm

My anxiety at being out of the house was made even worse by being with a beautiful woman.

All the old insecurities that had haunted my schooldays resurfaced. The general rule of thumb was this: the more attractive the girl, the less capable I was of talking coherently.

And Lori was the most attractive woman I had ever been out with.

Added to this was another complication. I was feeling seriously drowsy, and regretted not checking the dosage on the pack of R&R.

As if that wasn't enough, there was Cheyenne. Even though I'd taken an instant liking to her, I didn't have a clue how to talk to her.

To say conversation was stilted would be to imply there was conversation. It was the most agonising of painful small talk.

'So here we are,' I said, rubbing my hands in what was meant to convey a relaxed and confident manner.

'Yes, here we are,' said Lori, putting an end to that exchange.

A few minutes later I tried another tack.

'So…do they have restaurants like this in America?'

'What do you mean?' said Lori.

'Umm… I don't really know,' I admitted.

I then turned my attention to Cheyenne, thinking that if I could get her to like me, I'd have a better chance with her mother.

'So, Cheyenne. What have you been up to recently? Anything exciting happen?'

As soon as the words had left my mouth, I realised I'd said something incredibly stupid. After all, if running away to another country and leaving behind an abusive father wasn't a little out of the ordinary, what was?

'Trevor?' said Lori, interrupting my thoughts.

'Yes?'

'I'm kinda wondering if we're boring you. Only you keep yawning.'

'Oh, sorry. I'm just a little tired.' That sounded a lot better than explaining I'd taken an overdose of a herbal product called R&R.

'Do you mind if we go straight home after we've eaten, then? You know, I think we're gonna have an early night to get over the jet lag.'

 **Wed 8.58 pm**

As soon as Lori and Cheyenne had gone to bed, I went on to the Internet, found a chatroom where no one knew me, and put out a heartfelt plea.

'Can anyone help me?' I typed. 'I've just met a woman I really like but I'm finding it really hard to talk to her. Any advice would be very welcome.'

After a few seconds a message came up from Princess Leia.

'You came to the right place, Lord Brett,' she said. 'Why don't you start by telling me which galaxy you call home?'

'I'm an Earthling,' I typed, 'from a place called New Zealand.'

'Where does your woman live?'

'She lives with me.'

'She lives with you? And you don't know how to talk to her?'

'We met in a chatroom. She's from the States and she only arrived yesterday. It's not going well. Where are you from, Princess?'

'Johannesburg in South Africa.'

'And what do you do for a living?'

'I'm a graphic designer.'

'So you're stuck in front of a computer all day? I couldn't stand that. Still, it has to be better than trying to flog overpriced herbs that no one wants.'

'Ahh…you're a Herbal Solutions distributor?'

'I am. So tell me, have you ever met anyone online?'

'My last boyfriend.'

'What happened?'

'He met someone at a convention and cast me aside like a rusted 'droid. So — what did you guys talk about when you were chatting online?'

'Everything. How we felt, our lives, our problems. Now we're actually together, we can't seem to talk about anything.'

'You have to make her feel relaxed. She'll be feeling the pressure. Remember — she's the one in the strange country who has given everything up to be with you. Just don't have any expectations. For now, try and be her friend. It'll be worth it, I promise.'

'*Princess Leia, thanks for your help. Live long and prosper!*'
'*That's* Star Trek, *not* Star Wars.'
'*Sorry. Look, would you mind if I asked you for advice occasionally? I think I'm going to need it.*'
She gave me her e-mail address.

 Fri 3.22 am

The phone rang at just after three in the morning, so I immediately switched into Lord Brett mode.
I picked it up and gave a suave greeting. The voice at the other end was a familiar one.
'Where's my motherfucking wife, you asshole? I'll fucking kill you. I'll put a fucking bullet through your fucking brain.'
It was clear by now that this wasn't one of my cyberwomen. I let Arlen continue his rant.
'You want some? You want some of this, motherfucker?'
'Some of what?'
'This, you asshole.'
'I can't see you, Arlen. We're talking on the phone. I don't know what "this" is.'
'It's a fucking gun. Now you let me talk to my wife, or I'm coming over there and you're all gonna be fuckin' dead.'
'She's asleep. It's the middle of the night.'
'It ain't the middle of the night, you dumbass. You think I'm stupid? It's six pm. Hell, it ain't even dark yet, so you get that whore and you tell her she's gonna talk to me.'
'She doesn't want to.'
'Oh, she will want to when you hear what I've got to say. She took my daughter out of the country illegally, motherfucker. So now, we're gonna go to court to get her back where she belongs. Here with her dad. Her real family.'

# Sat 8.52 am

I told Lori about the late-night phone call over breakfast. If she was scared, she didn't show it.

I was scared and I did show it.

'Look, Lori, I'll quite understand if you tell me you have to go back.'

'You think I'm giving up on us this easy? You think I'm going back to him at the first sign of trouble. Jesus, Trevor, he's right about one thing.'

'What's that?'

'You really are an asshole.'

Sun 11.23 am

One problem I hadn't anticipated was chatroom withdrawal.

I'd experienced it before, of course, when the phone had been cut off. But I thought this would be different and that having Lori and Cheyenne around would more than make up for missing out on the Internet.

But we still weren't communicating the way we did before we met. And now there was the added stress of Arlen trying to get his daughter back. I didn't even know if he was serious or just trying to scare Lori.

I was trying to take Princess Leia's advice and not put any pressure on her.

After nearly a week together, things had begun to take on a pattern. Every day Lori would suggest going out for the day, and every day I would come up with an excuse.

It was only going to be a matter of time before I was found out.

Mon 10.29 am

Lori had just spoken the words I dreaded hearing.

'How's about we all have a day out in Wellington? Just you, me and Cheyenne? I figured we could visit the museum and go for a romantic walk along the beach and get to know each other. And I know how much you love romantic walks along the beach, Lord Brett.'

'Look, I'd love to, but I can't today. I've got a few things to do. Why don't you go without me and maybe we could grab a meal out later?'

'Sounds good.'

'I was thinking we could go to the Casablanca Café.'

'The place we went on Friday?'

'Yes, that's the one.'

She looked at me thoughtfully.

'Okay, then.'

They left for their day out and I went straight online, looking for Princess Leia. When I found her, I came right out with it.

'*Princess Leia, things may be a little worse than I let on. Thing is, I'm kind of housebound, and I haven't actually told Lori about this.*'

'*Mister, you got a problem.*'

'*What should I do?*'

'*There's only one thing you can do – tell her. So why are you housebound?*'

'*I don't really know. I just get panic attacks when I go out.*'

'*You ever try hypnotherapy?*'

'*Yup.*'

'*Counselling?*'

'*Yup.*'

'*Homeopathy? Reiki? Acupuncture?*'

'*Yup, yup, yup. And ear candles.*'

'*Do you have any idea what caused it?*'

'*I saw a naturopath and he reckoned it was because of mercury poisoning.*'

'*Oh, Okay, I've heard of that. So have you tried colonic irrigation?*'

'*Colonic what?*'

'*It's where you get your colon washed out by running warm water through it. In the States you're nobody unless you have regular colonics. Supposed to cure all kinds of things, especially anything to do with toxins.*'

'*How does the water get into the colon?*'

'*Through a tube.*'

'*And where does the tube go?*'

'*I think you can guess, Lord Brett.*'

 Mon 11.11 am

The bad news was that all the colonic practitioners in Wellington were outside my comfort zone.

The good news was that I found a place online that sold do-it-yourself colonic irrigation kits.

I immediately placed an order. It would take about a week to arrive from California.

Feeling full of new-found optimism, I decided to thank Princess Leia for all her help by getting her something *Star Wars*-related from eBay.

I found just what I was looking for. An original light sabre, as used in the original film by Luke Skywalker.

I put in an opening bid of $100 because I thought she was worth splashing out on. A couple of days later I checked in to see if I'd won. I hadn't. It had gone for more than $200 000.

I got her a small model of R2D2 instead.

 Mon 6.55 pm

The restaurant was exactly the same as it been a few days before. In fact, it hadn't changed in all the years I'd been going there.

I managed to get my favourite table – the one just by the door so that I could run out if I felt panicky.

Lori was still buzzing with excitement after her day in Wellington. She'd fallen in love with the city, with its quaint buildings, quirky shops and frankly deranged street entertainers.

This was looking promising for our long-term future. But I knew that before I could even think about the possibility of her staying, I had to admit everything.

'Lori, there's something I have to tell you.'

'Trevor, what is it?'

'I was going to keep going until you found out, but Princess Leia said I should get it out into the open.'

She looked alarmed.

'Trevor, what are you talking about? And who's Princess Leia?'
'You know – from Star Wars. It's not the real Princess Leia, obviously. She just calls herself that.'
'And she's what – some girlfriend you haven't told me about?'
'No, she's just a friend. Someone I talk to about how much I like you and how I have a secret that you're going to hate me for when I tell you.'
She looked me in the eye and slowly started to smile.
'This big secret – is it the fact you're agoraphobic?'
I looked at her in disbelief.
'How did you know?'
'It wasn't hard to work out, Trevor. Now can we order? I haven't eaten all day.'

 ## Tue 7.17 pm

It was like a dam had burst.

Conversation suddenly became a whole lot easier. Lori said that she couldn't really complain about me keeping secrets when she'd hidden the fact that she was still married when we first met online.

The other thing we talked about was work. I wasn't that keen on her working as a dancer, and she wasn't that keen on me selling Herbal Solutions products.

Her reasoning was that she'd had several friends who had signed up with the company and then got stuck with a load of stock.

Thinking of the stack of boxes at home, I could see her point.

We went home from the restaurant in a much happier frame of mind.

 ## Tue 11.05 pm

After putting Cheyenne to bed, Lori poured a couple of drinks and sat down beside me on the sofa.

She then moved closer and did something that sent a wave of electricity through me. She put her hand on my knee.

'Lori puts her hand on Lord Brett's knee,' she said, giggling.

I was quick to pick up on the game, putting my arm around her.

'Lord Brett seductively places his arm around Lori's slender shoulders and pulls her towards him.'

'Lori responds by kissing Lord Brett passionately.'

A few minutes later...

'Lord Brett starts to unbutton Lori's cardigan. He feels her firm breasts beneath the soft fabric of her blouse.'

'Lori removes Lord Brett's sweater and admires his *Ponch from CHiPS* T-shirt.'

'Lord Brett kisses Lori again, his tongue exploring her mouth.'

Actually, that bit was mumbled incoherently on account of the fact my tongue was in her mouth.

'Lori slowly takes Lord Brett's shirt off and runs her fingers across his broad, manly chest.'

I liked that bit.

'Lord Brett slowly unbuttons Lori's blouse, admiring her flat stomach and lacy bra.'

'Lori feels Lord Brett's hardness beneath his jeans.'

'Lord Brett unhooks Lori's bra to release her perfect breasts. He takes her nipple between his fingers.'

'Lori responds by undoing Lord Brett's jeans and pulling them off.'

'Lord Brett suddenly feels shy. How about he turns the light out?'

'Don't worry, Lord Brett – there's nothing of yours I haven't seen before.'

'There's nothing of mine your husband hasn't seen before either.'

And that was when the talking stopped and the frustration of not having physical contact with each other for all those long months was finally released.

 ## Wed 1.18 am

I was happy, Lori was happy and Princess Leia was happy.

Lori had gone off to get some sleep, but I was too excited, so had joined the Princess in our usual chatroom.

I told her that things had improved and that we were starting to get on as well offline as we had online.

She asked if I had a pic of the two of us and I promised I'd get one taken the next day.

I then asked if she had a photo of herself, since it seemed odd chatting away and not knowing what she looked like.

She said she'd e-mail one right away.

It arrived a few minutes later. I liked the look of her. She wore silver-framed, thick-lensed glasses and had 'doughnut-style' plaits on the sides of her head, much like the real Princess Leia.

She was wearing a *Star Wars* convention T-shirt, with *Ewoks* on it, and what I could see of her apartment was covered in *Star Wars* paraphernalia.

She looked a lot like Carrie Fisher did when she played Princess Leia in the first film.

Except, of course, Carrie Fisher wasn't middle-aged and she wasn't black.

 Fri 8.38 am

There was a little package in the mail, postmarked Tauranga.

I recognised Kate's handwriting and eagerly tore it open, wondering if she'd decided that getting together again wasn't such a bad idea.

Obviously, I was hoping for underwear, but wouldn't have been disappointed if it was photos.

It turned out to be neither.

The only thing in the package was a box of matches, including one that had been used.

It seemed that the mystery of who had tried to set fire to the flat was no longer a mystery.

 Fri 9.00 am

Lori had gone to town to look for a job, and we'd decided that Cheyenne would stay with me so that we could get to know each other.

This sounded fine in theory, but as soon as Lori left, a cloud of awkwardness settled over us and refused to budge. I just didn't have the slightest idea what to talk about. And she just looked at me expectantly

— which is pretty much what you'd expect from an eight-year-old.

Eventually, to the relief of both of us, she asked if she could use the Internet.

'Can't see why not. What do you want it for?'

'I like chatrooms.'

I was a little surprised.

'You did that when you were at home?'

'Sure. We all did.'

'Even your dad?'

'Especially my dad.'

An idea was starting to form.

 Fri 11.52 am

Once, when Maya and I were spending an evening together in the virtual sense, we learnt that an online friend suspected her online boyfriend was cheating on her.

She asked if one of us could come back into the room under a different name and test how faithful he was.

And that was how I became Hot Cali Chick.

Sure enough, he soon started privately whispering to me. This means that no one else but me could see what he was typing. Which was just as well, since the things he wanted to do to me were things no one had ever wanted to do to me before.

This included ripping off my cotton panties with his teeth, spanking my firm, tight ass and bringing me to a screaming climax with his tongue.

He asked me to send a picture, so I e-mailed him the one of me looking like Alan Rickman.

The resulting abuse was made more tolerable by watching him get dumped by his girlfriend in full view of everyone.

At the time, I didn't let on how much I enjoyed being someone else, but I always felt I'd like to do it again some time.

Fri 2.17 pm

When Lori returned from an unsuccessful day's jobhunting, I tried to find out a bit more about Arlen's chatroom activities.

'Trevor, when he's not on the couch, he's in his damn chatrooms. It's the only place women talk to him.'

'You didn't mind?'

'Mind? Hell, no. Meant I didn't have to be with his sorry ass. I think he even met up with some of them.'

'So you know which chatrooms he likes to go to?'

'Sure.'

'I'm thinking we could have a little fun with him...'

My plan was only half-baked at best, and didn't really have a point other than to confuse and cause him at least a fraction of the emotional turmoil he'd put his family through. Which was good enough for me and good enough for Lori.

What we were going to do was go to his favourite chatroom under an assumed female name (Ingrid) and make him fall for this non-existent girl.

Like I said, it hadn't really been thought out.

Chapter 6

Fri 10.25 am

I used to have a goldfish.

One day, I noticed it was getting a bit bloated, but I didn't really take much notice.

A couple of days later, it had blown up even bigger, and its middle was now the size of a ping-pong ball.

I rang the vet and was told that there was nothing that could be done. Twenty-four hours later my goldfish literally exploded.

It was only now, as I lay on my colonics board in the bathroom, legs up in the air, slowly filling my insides with warm water from a small plastic tube, that I was beginning to understand how the fish had felt.

I was so full I felt sure I would burst.

And still the water kept flowing into me until eventually, and to my great relief, it started flowing out.

The slow flow became a rapid stream before finally becoming the Niagara Falls.

I couldn't really see how this was supposed to stop me getting panic attacks every time I stepped outside, but decided to stick with it.

After all, celebrities all around the world swore by it.

Sat 10.11 pm

I couldn't have been asleep more than a few minutes before the phone woke me up again. Half expecting it to be Arlen, I tentatively picked it up.

'Hello?'

Much to my relief, the voice at the other end was female and American.

'Hello, Trevor?'

'Oh hi, how are you?' I said with enthusiasm. 'Have you finished for the day?'

It was my usual strategy of pretending to know who I was speaking to and then digging for clues.

'I'm fine, thank you.'

'That's great. Did you work hard today?'

This would let me know whether she worked or was still at school.

'Work was fine, thank you.'

'That's great. And um…look, I'm not sure if I got your last e-mail – can you remember what it was about?'

'Look, Trevor, I'd really like to speak to Lori. Could you put her on?'

Shit. This wasn't going well.

'Could I tell her who's calling?'

'It's Olivia Morgan, Lori's mother.'

'Oh, hi, Olivia. Nice to talk to you. I'll just go and get her.'

I found Lori looking wistfully out of the window.

'It's your mother,' I said, before adding needlessly, 'for you.'

She rushed to the phone and her side of the conversation was sprinkled with things like 'Oh, my God', 'Are you serious?' and 'That is so awesome'.

From what I could make out, Arlen had turned up at their house, drunk and tearful, pleading for the return of his big-screen TV. He was so desperate that he'd got down on his knees and begged, saying that he'd do anything they wanted.

Lori found the story so funny, she had tears running down her face. I realised this was the first time I'd seen her truly happy since she got here.

 **Sun 12.16 am**

Happiness is just as easy to convey in chatrooms as it is in real life.

There, people don't smile. Instead, they type out :)

They don't laugh. Instead they type LOL, which stands for 'Laughing Out Loud'.

They don't laugh hysterically. Instead they type ROTFL, which stands for 'Rolling On The Floor Laughing'.

And when they find something really, really amusing, they type LMAO. This is shorthand for 'Laughing My Ass Off'.

The ultimate is a combination of the last two. This is reserved for something so amusing that it causes near-death convulsions. ROTFLMAO or, you guessed it, 'Rolling On The Floor Laughing My Ass Off'.

All of this makes faking it a whole lot easier. You can be sitting there looking (and feeling) totally miserable, yet all you have to do is type any of the above and whoever you're talking to will think you're appreciative company.

There are obnoxious acronyms for everything. From the short-and-to-the-point 'K', meaning 'okay' or 'all right', to the long-winded 'IYKWIMAITYD', which means 'If You Know What I Mean And I Think You Do'.

Ironically, the only time I ever used the latter, the person I was chatting to (Banana Fairy, if memory serves me right) had no idea what I meant.

 Mon 10.06 am

Lori was delivering on a long-term promise to take Cheyenne to the zoo, so I was left by myself.

I couldn't help feeling left out, even though I couldn't possibly have gone with them. So before long I was spilling my heart to Princess Leia.

'Lord Brett. Pray tell how is the romance going with the young maiden?'

'It's going great.'

'That's good.'

'By great, I mean not very well.'

'Oh, I see. Want to talk about it?'

'Well, it's like she doesn't really want to be with me, but feels she has to. If I'm being honest, we don't really get on as well as we used to. Before we met.'

'So what do you do all day?'

'I watch TV and she does things with Cheyenne – her daughter. It's like *we have separate lives.'*

'May I ask a personal question?'

'Go ahead.'

'Do you sleep together?'

'No. Well, we did once.'

'Has she given any signals about what might be making her unhappy?'

'No, I don't think so. Although she did say that she hated having no social life, what with me not going out.'

'Oh.'

'Could that be a problem?'

'Yeah, of course.'

'So what can I do?'

'Are you getting any better yet? Did you try that colonic irrigation?'

'I've had a couple of sessions, but not feeling any effects just yet.'

'Hey, I've got an idea.'

'What is it?'

'Well, you can't go out, right?'

'Right.'

'So *throw a dinner party in her honour. Invite your friends over to meet her. She'll love it.'*

What a great idea! I suddenly felt I could do something that would bring Lori and me closer together.

It was only when I realised I had hardly any friends that the elation faded.

Wed 8.20 am

It was as though Lori suddenly had a purpose in life. The dinner party was going to be her chance to meet my friends and make some friends of her own.

She took charge of the menu, writing out recipes and shopping lists with an enthusiasm she'd never shown towards me.

I couldn't really admit to how few friends I had, so I decided to invite Bernie, as well as a couple of people I'd met online. More specifically, Leanne (who only lived a couple of streets away), LadyDay22 (I didn't know her real name), Hannah (of asparagus farmer fame) and Scott (who had flown to LA to be with a woman who didn't want him). They all lived in Wellington, and I'd known them all long enough to get away with asking them.

 Thu 3.32 pm

I saw Kate only one more time after getting her little package. It was in a magazine article about Internet dating. She was pictured with a smiling, shaven-headed man in his thirties, who had his arm around her. They were looking into each other's eyes and seemed to be sharing a joke.

She looked good. Gone were the Dame Edna glasses and the severe hairstyle.

I skimmed through the article until I came to her bit:

I've definitely had to kiss a few frogs before finding my prince,'
said Kate, twenty-four, from Tauranga. 'I met up with a couple of
guys through the Internet, but they turned out to be total losers.
One of them was really boring. He just had no personality and as
soon as we met he was all over me, trying to paw me.

I resented that. First, I thought we got on pretty well. And second, she was a willing participant in all the pawing that went on. As I carried on reading, I discovered she hadn't been talking about me at all:

The other guy was even worse. He totally lied about his appearance,
his age, everything. He turned out to be borderline obese and had a
repulsive rash on his leg. It was horrible. That's why I'd recommend to
any woman reading this who has been tempted to look for love online
to thoroughly check out the guy before meeting him, and always make
the first date in a public place. When I met Carlos for the first time, it
was for lunch at a café on the waterfront. There was an instant spark
between us and it just went from there. We're planning a June
wedding, so to all those doubters out there, we're living proof that you
can find love on the Internet.

Unless I was very much mistaken, the 'other guy' she referred to was me.

Tue 5.22 pm

We developed Ingrid's character and life story based on Lori's description of Arlen's ideal woman.

We decided to use the picture Jacqui had originally sent me when I was starting out on my chatroom life – the Glamor Shot® that showed a blonde with big tits in a blue sequinned dress.

Like Jacqui and Lori, Ingrid worked as a stripper, the difference being that Ingrid lived in South Africa. The reason for locating her there was so we could get Princess Leia to post him little presents, supposedly from Ingrid.

Lori was sure Arlen would fall for her. After all, she liked guns, country and western music, and Southern Comfort. She watched *Jerry Springer*, *Days of Our Lives* and WWF wrestling.

She read the *National Enquirer* and nothing else.

In her spare time, she liked to go fishing or just hang out in bars – wearing very little.

Frankly, I quite fancied her myself.

 Mon 4.45 pm

Apart from Arlen, my other pressing problem was money.

I was now ready to admit that Herbal Solutions wasn't going to do for me what it did for Ted DiMarco, Alan Mitchell and Luanne Irving, while Lori had taken one look at Wellington's 'gentlemen's clubs' and decided that they weren't for her.

While in town, she'd had an idea. After browsing around several antique shops and thinking that the prices were a lot less than she expected, she decided that Americans would happily pay more.

Her scheme was to buy up historic artefacts, such as maps, documents and antique furniture, on the cheap, then put them on eBay. Brilliant!

We decided that she would go back early the next morning and buy up a few items so we could do a test run.

🧑 Wed 9.19 pm

I was sitting in front of the computer and Lori was leaning over my shoulder.
We'd been in the Tennessee Chatroom, under the name of Ingrid.
Plenty of men tried to strike up a conversation, but there was only one man Ingrid was interested in. And right on cue, he appeared.

His screen name was The Phantom.

Even though he was thousands of miles away, my pulse quickened. He still scared me, but I didn't want Lori to know.

Lori explained that he had named himself after his favourite comic book character.

It wasn't long before he made his move, which was a whispered message to Ingrid.

'Hi darlin :)'

Ingrid didn't reply straight away. We didn't want him to be suspicious. Undeterred, he tried again.

'So howz ur day bin :) ?'

It was time for Ingrid to reply.

'Same old same old.'

The Phantom shot back with:

'A/S/L?'

He wanted to know Ingrid's age, sex and location.

'I'm 23, female, 5' 6", weigh 115 pounds, live in Joburg, South Africa. U?''28, 6'2" and 220 pounds. Got a place in Greensboro, North Carolina.'

Ignoring the fact that he'd lost four years in age, gained five inches in height and sixty pounds in weight, Ingrid continued.

'Southern man, huh?'

'LOL. U got a bf?'

He wanted to know if she had a boyfriend.

'No. U got a gf?

'Not right now :)'

'Ever been married?'

'No way.'

'LOL.'

'*U?*'

'*Was married. Kicked her ass to the curb.*'

Lori started giggling helplessly. She told me to ask him what happened, so I did.

'*She never did nuthin round the house. Used to lay on the couch drinking all day while I worked. U got a job?*'

'*I dance at a club. U?*'

'*Got me a Harley Davidson dealership.*'

Hearing a snort of hysterical laughter, I looked behind me.

Lori was literally ROTFL.

 # Fri 11.03 am

Lori, Cheyenne and I were going out. Our destination was the local supermarket, which was like a small-scale version of a proper supermarket. We were there to buy everything on Lori's list for the dinner party.

It felt like being part of a real family, doing something that real families do. Pushing the trolley around, throwing things in.

Suddenly Lori stopped and looked at me suspiciously.

'Why are you walking funny?'

'I'm not.'

'Yes, you are, Trevor. You're strutting. You normally walk with a kind of slouch.'

It slowly dawned upon me why. The music coming from the speakers was *Night Fever* by the Bee Gees. The song at the beginning of *Saturday Night Fever*.

I blushed and went back to slouching.

Lori was determined to impress my friends and make the dinner party a huge success. She bought ice cream, sparkling wine, snacks, candles, prime cuts of meat, fresh vegetables, cheese.

It meant that there was something for everyone, even those on the Atkins Diet (the diet that was actually working for me, against all expectations).

There was a set of scales at the mall that, bizarrely, gave you a printout of your horoscope as well as your weight for $1. Since my own scales were now tucked away under the stairs gathering dust (alongside the solar-powered alarm clock, Ab Cruncher and several other malfunctioning, NASA-developed pieces of equipment – I was just glad I wasn't an astronaut), I had a regular weekly weigh-in at the mall.

Since starting the diet four weeks ago, I had lost eighteen pounds and got four hopelessly inaccurate horoscopes, none of which warned me about the $235.35 I had to hand over at the checkout.

Still, Lori was really glowing and I remember thinking, 'It doesn't get any better than this'.

As it turned out, I was right. It didn't.

 ## Tue 3.25 pm

Lori's next shopping expedition was even more expensive.

She spent five hours trudging from antique shop to antique shop before settling on a framed painting of a moana bird from the 1800s entitled *Te Kete Moana*, a postcard from 1907 wishing Happy Christmas to a Mrs Kew in Pokono, and an art deco coat-hanger that had a hook in the form of a gecko.

The total cost was $255.

We put them all up on eBay and waited for the offers to come flooding in from wealthy American collectors.

I also put up for sale twenty-eight boxes of various herbal remedies, which I was a lot less confident of unloading, as well as one barely used Ab Cruncher, one barely used set of scales and one barely used solar-powered alarm clock.

 ## Wed 07.30 am

I woke early the following morning, without the benefit of an alarm clock, and rushed into the living room so I could see what bids had come through.

Lori was already sitting at the computer and she looked excited.

'We've had bids on everything,' she announced. 'The painting's already up to US $200, which means we've already covered what we spent.

The postcard and hanger are both over US $50. I can't believe it.'

'That's brilliant. When do the auctions close?'

'Another week. So we've got seven days for the prices to get even higher. Lord Brett, I do declare we are on to something here.'

'Great! Oh, by the way, any offers for the other stuff?'

'No.'

She looked at her watch.

'And now it's time that Ingrid went to meet The Phantom.'

 Wed 7.42 am

The Phantom pounced the second Ingrid arrived in the chatroom.

'*Hey,*' he whispered into her cyber ear.

'*Hey yourself,*' replied Lori, whose turn it was to be Ingrid.

'*I bin thinkin bout u.*'

'*What kind of things have you been thinking?*'

'*U wouldn't wanna no.*'

'*LOL*'

'*Got a pic?*'

'*Only if u send me 1 first*'

'*Sure. I'll post it in here. BRB*'

A picture then appeared on the screen that had Lori laughing so much, I had to take over being Ingrid.

The image looked as though it had been torn from one of those aftershave ads in *GQ*. You could even see the tear mark around the side. A bronzed Adonis was gazing thoughtfully into the distance, pointing at something. His muscles glistened, his six-pack rippled and his teeth sparkled.

'Just play along with it,' said Lori, trying to catch her breath between bursts of giggling.

She'd once told me that Arlen had met up with a few women that he'd met on the Internet. I wondered how they could possibly have recognised him.

'*WOW!!! U R HOT!!!*' I typed.

'*I guess,*' he replied modestly. '*So now do I get 2 c yr pic?*'

'*Sure.*'

I got the glamour shot of Jacqui and posted it in the chatroom. His response was predictable.

'WOW!!!! U R HOT 2!!!!!'

'Why thank u, kind sir.'

'Do u like being a stripper?'

'It's OK, I spose. NE way, I'm an exotic dancer, not a stripper per se,' I replied, remembering something Jacqui (on whom Ingrid was modelled) had once told me.

'Sorry.'

'So how's business?'

'Huh?'

'Business. Your Harley dealership,' I reminded him, since he had evidently forgotten.

'Oh yeh, goin gr8. I sold like fifteen motorcycles today.'

'Fifteen. Hey, that's somethin else. Look, I gotta go 2 work. Bye.'

'Hey wait. Can u meet me here later?'

'No. But cum bak this time 2 moro. I'm worth waitin for.'

'I wanna send u sumthing. Can I have your e-mail?'

'Sure.'

I gave him the e-mail address we'd set up and Ingrid left the room.

 # Thu 10:22 am

There was an e-mail waiting for me from LadyDay22.

She would be glad to come to the dinner party, but first she wanted to know what food was being served because she was:

a. Allergic to shellfish.
b. Gluten intolerant.
c. Lactose intolerant, but could occasionally tolerate goat products.
d. Sugar was also a big no-no.

In addition, she wanted to know what, if any, alcohol was going to be available, since she also had a problem with preservatives.

The final request she had was to be seated nearest the door.

 **Thu 10.26 am**

A matter of minutes later an e-mail arrived from Arlen to Ingrid. He'd decided to woo her with poetry, and the poem he'd sent had a familiar look to it.

My darling rose who is my life
You make me complete
You are the only one for me
I bow at your feet.

It was exactly the same as a poem he'd sent Lori, but with the reference to Cheyenne taken out.

Lori was more upset than amused. Not because she was no longer the only one for him, but because of the way his daughter had been so callously deleted from his life.

 Fri 8.33 pm

Princess Leia was impressed with Lori's entrepreneurial efforts, but said it sounded almost like she seemed to prefer being my business partner than any other kind of partner.

I had to admit she had a point.

My big hope was the dinner party. It was now less than a week away and preparations were going well. The menu had been altered to suit LadyDay22's requirements, and Leanne, Scott and Hannah had all e-mailed to say they'd love to come.

Bernie had said he might not be able to make it as he was getting back from Singapore on the morning of the party, but I was confident he'd be there. Especially when he found out that three of the women didn't have boyfriends.

As for the fourth, Lori, I wasn't sure if she considered me her boyfriend or not – and I was too scared to ask her.

🧔 Fri 9.00 pm

The Phantom was in a romantic mood.

'Got a fever burning inside of me,' he said. 'You're driving me wild.'

I turned to Lori. 'Blimey, he's coming on a bit strong.'

'That's from his favourite song. He used to make me listen to it all the time. Fucking horrible.'

'What is it?'

'Hot Blooded by Foreigner.'

I typed a reply from Ingrid.

'Hey, I love that song. I'm a huge Foreigner fan. Have you got the album?'

'Sure.'

'Me too. Hey, let's both put the song on while we chat. It'll be kinda romantic.'

'Great. I'll just get the CD. BRB'

He was telling me he'd be right back, and sure enough, he was.

'You still there, Ingrid? You listening to it? Cos I am.'

'Yeah. Listening to it and lovin' it. So why don't you tell me a bit more about yourself? All I know is that you have a Harley dealership, you're divorced and that you're hotter 'n hell.'

'Wot u want 2 no?'

'What you like to do in your spare time?'

'I like wrestling. WWF. And I like long walks on the beach.'

'Hey, I'm a WWF fan, too. Who's your favourite wrestler?'

'Nature Boy Ric Flair. He's awesome, dude.'

'I like the Hulkster.'

'Hogan? No way. I love that guy.'

'Saw him at Summerslam.'

'You have gotta be the perfect woman.'

'Are you flirting with me, Phantom?'

'Would you like it if I was?'

'Definitely.'

'So what else do you want to know? C'mon, ask me anything you want.'

'Got any kids?'

'Kids? No, have you?'

'Yeah, I've got a little girl. She's perfect. Her dad has no interest in her, though. Can you believe that?'

'I don't get that. I mean, kids are great, right?'

'Right.'

 # Sat 2.45 am

I couldn't wait until the next morning to see how the eBay auctions were going. I was too excited to sleep.

I got up at 2.35 and crept down to the computer. I logged on, signed in and couldn't believe my eyes when I saw what was going on.

Somewhere in America a person who went under the name of Wheelerdealer23 had put in a bid of $550 for the painting. $550! That was around seven times what we'd paid for it.

The postcard and hanger had both gone over US $100.

But that wasn't the most exciting thing. There was even a bid for my leftover herbal stock. It was only $50, but at least it was a start.

 # Sat 4.46 am

I checked again a couple of hours later.

Wheelerdealer23 had been outbid by Angus_beef, who wanted to buy the painting for $625. It was a bidding war.

 # Sat 6.12 am

Two hours after that Wheelerdealer23 had come back with an improved offer of $650.

Surely Angus_beef wasn't going to give in so easily?

I sat and stared at the screen, all thoughts of sleep having long since departed.

Sat 7.30 am

While I was waiting for more auction news, I checked the e-mail. There was another one from Arlen.

It seemed he'd fallen for the lovely but non-existent Ingrid. He wrote:

I've never felt this way about anyone before. It's like we've known each other our entire lives. I want to be with you for the rest of my life. Can I call you sometime?
Or maybe you could call me?
Hugs and kisses
Arlen (The Phantom)
Xxxooooxxxx

He then went on to ruin the effect by attaching a poem he'd written for her.

I want to buy you roses
To show how much I care
I want to give you a diamond ring
I want my life with you to share

Arlen was clearly in love. And I suspected Ingrid was going to feel the same way.

Sat 7.32 am

I also had an e-mail from LadyDay22.

'*Dear Lord Brett,*' she wrote, clearly unwilling to cross the line into the real world just yet. '*I'm really looking forward to Friday. I have attached, just to clarify, a list of foods that could potentially contain gluten. I also just wanted to check that you will have vegan food available.*'

Vegan? This was the first I'd heard of it. Considering I lived on nothing but animal products, it's not something I would have considered.

But Lori had. She'd thought of everything. And there would be something for everyone, whatever their tastes.

Sat 8.45 am

Apparently Angus_beef couldn't stand the heat and had dropped out of the bidding. But the disappointment of that was tempered by the emergence of a new player from the cybershadows, known only as The_China_Doll, who had waited until the last possible moment to enter the auction.

Hers turned out to be the winning bid.

Which meant that Lori and I had just sold a $200 painting of a bird for $675.

Sat 3.55 pm

'*So, what's it like in Joburg?*' asked Arlen, as we chatted away that afternoon.

Shit. I had no idea. Luckily, inspiration struck. Opening another window on the computer, I did a quick Google search, scanned through the information, then adapted it.

'*Well, it generates 16 percent of South Africa's GDP and employs 12 percent of the national workforce. Our financial, municipal, roads and telecommunications infrastructure matches leading first world cities, yet the cost of living is far lower. The World Economic Forum rates the banking sector the sixth most sophisticated in the world.*'

'*Damn girl, you know your shit. So what do y'all do for fun at night?*'

Back to Google. Less than a minute later...

'*Party animals agree that when it comes to nightlife, Jo'burg rocks. The city buzzes with an exciting range of dance clubs and a live music scene that's renowned the world over. South African jazz is particularly popular, and there are many sophisticated venues where you can get down and experience the rhythm and soul of Africa.*'

'*Jazz is kinda cool, but it ain't* Foreigner, *if you know what I'm sayin'.*'

'That's for sure.'

That's for sure? That was an expression used by Swedish tennis players, wasn't it? Not South African strippers.

'So what other Foreigner songs do you like as well as Hot Blooded?'

Okay, now I was in trouble. Lori was out buying antiques and my knowledge of *Foreigner* was limited to the knowledge that they were a bland 1980s, radio-friendly band with big hair who churned out forgettable songs.

Once again, Google came to the rescue.

'Well, I guess the one I always wanted played at my wedding is I Want to Know What Love Is.*'*

My wedding? The only place I'd ever hear that song played was the supermarket. I continued with my list of *Foreigner* favourites.

'I also love Cold as Ice, Urgent, Juke Box Hero, Waiting for a Girl Like You, Double Vision *and* Head Games.

'Wow, that's AWESOME. So what other bands do you like?'

Lori came through the door at just the right moment, her arms full of bric-a-brac.

'The Phantom wants to know what kind of music Ingrid likes, apart from Foreigner.'

'Guns and Roses, Bon Jovi and Boston,' Lori said.

'Guns and Roses, Bon Jovi *and* Boston,' I typed.

'Ingrid darlin'?' The Phantom said.

'Yes, babe?'

'You are too good to be true'.

 ## Sat 4.44 pm

Lori's trip to the various antique shops had produced the following:

1 hand-carved Maori mask representing Patupaearehe, the king of the fairy folk.

1 Wanganui and District telephone directory from 1932.

1 Carpet wall hanging of Mount Taranaki.

1 New Zealand Gas Corporation ashtray, circa 1950.

1 New Zealand number plate 1936.

Dave Roberts

This was going to bring in a fortune on eBay, and Lori had spent just $720 on the whole lot.

That wasn't the only cause for optimism either.

After weighing myself earlier (down to 220 pounds), the horoscope said that *Your business ideas come to fruition. Something you have been planning for a long time is a great success.*

 ## Fri 8.40 am

The sound of the phone interrupted my dream, which, from what I could remember, was about Lori climbing into bed with me.

I glanced at the clock. It was 8.40. Why would anyone ring me at this hour? I soon found out.

'Mr Niblock?'

'Speaking.'

'This is Mr Duthie's surgery. You had an appointment at 8.30.'

Shit. Of all the ideal pre-dinner party scenarios, being late for a dentist who was going to remove the fillings from several teeth, without using anaesthetic, was pretty low down on the list.

I dragged myself out of bed, put on a clean Pokemon T-shirt and ran to the waiting Mr Duthie.

'Sorry I'm late. I've got a dinner party tonight.'

I have no idea why I said that. It didn't make sense. I put it down to a combination of nerves and wanting to show off that I had a social life – even if it was for one night only.

He sat me down, got me to open my mouth and peered myopically inside.

'This could be tricky,' was all he said, before proceeding to subject me to previously unimaginable levels of pain.

But as I lay there, I had a brainwave. Perhaps it was the body's way of forcing me to refocus, but there and then I came up with the perfect way to make Arlen suffer as much as I was.

I couldn't wait to tell Lori.

Fri 10.18 am

I rushed home to find her cooking about five things at once. Her assistant, Cheyenne, was setting the table.

I immediately felt surplus to requirements.

'Can I do anything?' I asked.

Lori shook her head.

'Everything's under control.'

'Lori, I just had a brainwave. This is totally brilliant.'

I caught my reflection in the window. I was waving my arms around, looking deranged with excitement.

'Can't it wait?'

'No. Listen. I finally worked out how we get even with Arlen. You know he would do anything for Ingrid? Well, we get her, or rather Princess Leia pretending to be her, to call him and persuade him to visit her. In South Africa.'

Lori looked at me blankly.

'And this is the best bit. We tell him to wear his White Power T-shirt, then get him to meet her in one of the townships.'

In my head, sitting in the dentist's chair, the plan had sounded ingenious. Now, coming out of my mouth, it sounded totally rubbish.

She didn't have to point out the many flaws. She just looked at me and said, 'Yeah, great, now can I get on with getting your dinner party ready?'

I caught another glimpse of myself in the window on the way out. My head was bowed and my arms were no longer flapping.

 # Fri 4.12 pm

I got a phone call from Leanne.

She wouldn't be able to make it because she'd met the perfect man last night and he was flying out from Australia to be with her.

Coming from anyone else, this would have sounded like a far-fetched excuse to get out of coming to the dinner party.

Coming from Leanne, I knew it would be true.

His name was Shane, and he'd been working the mines in Kalgoorlie to make enough money to set up his own courier business.

They'd already discussed buying a house together in Wellington and running the business from home.

I had no doubt whatsoever that he'd be on his way back where he came from within a few weeks. Just like all the others.

Still, there was one good thing about Leanne not coming. We'd now have an even split, with three women and three men. Provided, of course, that Bernie and Scott showed up.

 ## Fri 7.10 pm

I thought I heard a knocking on the door, but then decided I must have been imagining it. After all, neither Lori or Cheyenne seemed to have noticed anything.

A couple of minutes later, I heard it again. A slight tapping sound, like a small bird pecking wood.

I went to investigate and opened the door.

An overweight woman in her late thirties was standing there, shaking. Her dress sense seemed to have been strongly influenced by *Dr Who* circa 1975. She had a long scarf, big coat, which was unbuttoned, and a hat that defied description. She looked as though it was taking a tremendous effort to force herself to speak.

Eventually she did.

'Lord Brett Sinclair?'

She thrust out her glove-covered hand.

'LadyDay22. I am honoured to meet thee, kind sir.'

 ## Fri 7.12 pm

I introduced LadyDay22 to Lori and Cheyenne, and we all sat down.

'May I take your coat?'

'Not just yet, if you don't mind.'

The awkward conversation was thankfully interrupted by another knock on the door, this time a loud and confident one.

I opened it and couldn't believe my eyes.

 ## Fri 7:13 pm

Hannah was standing there.

I knew it was her because she was exactly the way she described herself. What's more, she looked exactly like her photo.

This was unprecedented. Someone from the Internet who had been totally truthful about their appearance.

She really was around 5' 6" and slim, with shoulder-length auburn hair. Her photo must have been taken recently, which is almost unheard of in cyberworld.

She'd even been truthful when she told me she looked a bit like Uma Thurman. I'd stopped taking such claims seriously when a supposed Christina Applegate lookalike from Minnesota sent me a photo showing a 200-pound tattooed blonde, who looked less like Christina Applegate than I do.

I could see by the expression on Hannah's face that she wasn't totally impressed with how my description of myself measured up to the reality.

 ## Fri 7:35 pm

That was the last time anyone knocked on the door that night. (I later learnt that Bernie was too jetlagged to come, and that Scott couldn't tear himself away from his current online affair.) This meant that Lori's dinner party for six had become a dinner party for four.

Times like this are a true test of character. You can either try and make the best out of a bad situation, or you can stand by helplessly while things deteriorate.

I stood by and watched helplessly as four people with nothing in common struggled to find common ground.

I was even quieter than usual. This was because my habit of drying up when in the presence of a beautiful woman was magnified due to being in the presence of two beautiful women.

On top of that, LadyDay22 looked incredibly uncomfortable and hadn't said a word since declining my offer to take her coat.

When she finally did speak, it was to ask if she could check her e-mail. Glad of something to do, I escorted her to the computer and went online, before leaving her to it.

Lori and Hannah had finally found some common ground. They were talking about me. I only caught the end of the conversation, but it made my heart sink.

I was pretty sure Hannah had asked Lori if she'd ever go back to the States, and Lori had said she'd be going back soon.

Much as she liked it here, the romance thing just hadn't worked out.

Fri 07.55 pm

The evening went from bad to worse.

When I went to tell LadyDay22 that dinner was about to be served, I found that she'd finished checking her e-mail and had moved on to the chatroom. She looked as though leaving the computer was the last thing she wanted to do, as she was involved in a chat with LordDay, her cyberhusband. He and I had fallen out a few months back over which of us was the first to call himself 'lord' and we hadn't spoken since.

She reluctantly typed her farewell and followed me to the dining table. Just as she was about to sit down, she suddenly announced that she had changed her mind and had to go home now and that she hoped that was okay.

I suspected she couldn't wait to get back to the more comfortable world of her favourite chatrooms.

I wished I could join her.

Fri 8.10 pm

LadyDay22 managed to get as far as the door before Lori called out to her in what I recognised as her calm-sounding-but-really-very-angry voice.

'Excuse me, but are you going somewhere? Only dinner's about to be served.'

'Well, I was going home. I did tell Lord Brett and he said it was okay.'

'Two things, honey. One, he's not fucking Lord Brett, his name's Trevor. And two, you are going nowhere until you've eaten this meal I've spent all day cooking, after spending God knows how long finding all your special ingredients.'

LadyDay22 looked at me, but I looked away.

'Well, I guess I could. But are you sure there's no gluten or dairy? Plus, if there's even a trace of preservative, I'll probably, like, die.'

'You have to be real careful how you eat, do you?' asked Lori.

LadyDay22 nodded her head sadly, as though silently contemplating the burden of living under such barbaric constraints.

'No burgers, chips or Coke?'

'I can't have anything like that.'

'How about cakes then? Or chocolate?'

'Oh, no. Never!'

'Then how come you weigh about 500 fucking pounds?'

There was a shocked silence.

LadyDay22 stood up with all the dignity she could muster and pushed past me, screaming something along the lines of how she wasn't going to be spoken to like that and she was going home.

I then heard a whimpering sound from across the room, and saw Hannah huddled in the corner, crying. 'I'm sorry, but I just can't handle this,' she said when I asked her if she was okay. 'I'd like to go home.' Lori replied with the word 'Fine', and Hannah scurried off, probably traumatised for life.

At least her fragile temperament explained why she preferred to live her life online. Just then Cheyenne came into the room, doubtless woken by all the shouting.

'Is there anything to eat, Mom? I'm starving.'

'Yes, hon,' replied her mother. 'There's plenty to eat. Help yourself.'

Sat 7.21 am

You can sometimes sense a house is empty, even before you take a look around. And that's how I knew Lori and Cheyenne had gone when I woke up around ten the morning after the disaster that was my dinner party.

They must have left in the middle of the night and would probably be somewhere over the Pacific by now.

I spent the day in bed.

The only thing that got me up that night wasn't hunger or a decision to get on with the rest of my life.

It was because I hadn't checked my e-mail in nearly ten hours.

 # Sat 3.15 pm

I had sixteen e-mails waiting for me, none of them urgent.

By contrast, the fictional Ingrid had forty-three in her inbox, every one of them from Arlen, every one pleading with her to contact him.

All the revenge ideas I'd had suddenly paled into insignificance when I realised that there was one thing that would cause him more anguish than anything else.

That would be if Ingrid simply disappeared and never contacted him again. The more I thought about this, the more I liked it.

 # Sat 8.12 pm

I got an urgent phone call from Leanne.

Apparently Shane from Kalgoorlie was really starting to get on her nerves and she wanted to get rid of him. Could I possibly come round pretending to be her ex-boyfriend who she loved very much and wanted to get back with?

I wearily got my coat, hoping that he wasn't bigger than me.

 **Sun 12.22 am**

I made a vow to myself.

No more chatrooms. Ever.

That part of my life was over. It was for losers. There were other more normal ways to meet women, and it was time to move on.

Move on to online personal ads.

There were literally thousands of sites to choose from. Vegetarian Singles, Chubby Singles, Graduate Singles, Jewish Singles.

I decided to choose one at random by typing 'online personals' into Google and going with whatever came seventh in the list. That was how I found myself at okcupid.com.

This was even better than chatrooms. Here you could look through page after page of women, taking your time to carefully select the one you wanted to spend the rest of your life with.

I eventually narrowed it down to two, whose beauty made them stand out from the crowd. VOICE OF AN ANGLE and 2HOT4U.

Chapter 7

 ## Mon 3.47 pm

The greatest personal ad of all time, and the standard by which all others must be measured was this, from some American magazine in the mid-1990s:

> *Bitter, unsuccessful middle-aged loser wallowing in an unending sea of inert, drooping loneliness looking for 24-year-old needy, leech-like hanger-on to abuse with dull stories, tired sex and Herb Alpert albums.*

It don't know how many replies it got, but it was in a different class from the ones I was reading, which were generally along the lines of this:

> *Anyone out there 4 a chat?*
> *Im kinda shy but once i get 2 no sum1 i open up i do consider myself as a fun lovin person.*

 ## Mon 7.54 pm

Before I was allowed to browse the women's ads, I had to come up with one of my own.

I researched the subject thoroughly and found that the ones that got most replies were from men with a bachelor's degree or better, who drank occasionally but didn't smoke, and were okay with one or two children.

There were a few constants in most of the ads I looked at.

a. Almost everyone was sick of the bar scene.
b. Very few didn't say that they were just as comfortable in a ballgown/tuxedo as they were in jeans.
c. And those long walks on the beach that were so popular in chatroom world also had a strong following in personal ad world.

As well as that, I had found yet another world of annoying acronyms.

Everyone wanted someone with a GSOH, which was a 'Good Sense Of Humour'. While the more discerning seekers of love specified NLP, or 'No Losers Please'.

But the one I hated most and vowed never to use, no matter how desperate I got, was WHPH.

It meant that the person liked to 'Work Hard and Play Hard'.

 # Mon 8.14 pm

My ad read:

> *I'm the total package!*
> *I love the bar scene so much I could never get sick of it. I feel really uncomfortable in a tuxedo, which is why I have had the same jeans for the past four years. I live on the sofa, so hate any kind of walks on the beach. I have no sense of humour (NSOH), and the age I've filled in bears no resemblance to my real age. I would really appeal only to those with a psychological condition that makes them seek out losers.*

The thinking behind this was that since no one would possibly answer it, I could look through women's ads without distraction.

That's what I told myself, anyway. The truth was that I couldn't see how anything I wrote could possibly get anyone to reply.

Tue 11:25 am

The next day I got an e-mail from the personal ad site.

It said that my ad had been accepted, but if I wanted to increase my replies by up to 80 per cent, all I had to do was add a photo.

That was easy for them to say.

Still, the Alan Rickman photo had had one or two positive comments, so I decided to put it up.

The next day I checked in and there it was. My ad was there for the world to see, and so was my photo.

Now I just had to wait.

Wed 11.13 pm

When you ask someone on the Internet for a photo, you soon learn to keep your expectations low.

Maybe one in ten people will send you an accurate likeness of the way they are. The rest will send one of the following:

- A photo taken years ago, when that person was 'maybe five pounds lighter' or when they had 'a bit more hair'.
- A driving licence picture (if American).
- A close-up of a body part, usually the eye or mouth or whatever the person considers their best feature.
- A group shot, where they omit to tell you which one is them. One thing you can be sure of, though. If the shot is of three women, they will always be doing the *Charlie's Angels* pose.
- A blurry shot, like that one of the Loch Ness Monster, except in these you can just about make out a human form.
- And then there were those who sent an old black and white picture that they are convinced makes them look like Alan Rickman.

Fri 6.16 pm

At last there was a reply to my ad.

This was the moment I'd been waiting for. After several days of humiliating silence, of checking in at least twenty times a day, a woman had actually plucked me from the vast ocean of desperate men.

I quickly made my way to her profile.

Okay, so she wasn't my type.

She wasn't a glamorous exotic dancer, but more of a homely, Caroline Quentin lookalike, with a chubby, friendly face, brownish hair and matching eyes.

She was also much older than I'd hoped for. So old, in fact, that she was exactly the same age as me.

Her message was brief and to the point.

Write to me now, Sinclair. Remember – ridicule is nothing to be scared of, and I should know. I've been on this fucking site for two months and have had nothing but one-line replies from idiots who think that sending pictures of their cock is an effective seduction technique and that 'Wassup?' is a compelling conversation opener.

At least you seem able to string a sentence together. Well, you didn't think I replied to your ad because of your photo, did you?

Write soon

e-luv

 # Fri 6.21 pm

e-luv? What kind of name was that?

And why had she quoted *Adam and the Ants*?

Although I didn't really fancy her, she did sound as though she could be quite amusing, so I decided to write back.

Fri 6.33 pm

Dear e-luv,

Thank you for your e-mail, which I plucked from literally thousands of replies to my ad.
Why did I pick you?
Because I don't think you're being entirely honest with me. I am not convinced that e-luv is your real name.
Of course, I use my real name.

Regards
Lord Brett Sinclair

 # Sun 8.12 am

Sinclair!
That is not your real name, you lying bastard. Even though Danny Wilde was the true star of The Persuaders, *at least Lord Brett used his social advantages to make the world a better place.*
As you so rightly guessed, e-luv is not my real name, although up until the age of four, I was convinced it was.
My real name is Charlotte. Blame my dad for this. He had a bookshop here in Brontë country, which I now run. And yes, before you ask, my sisters are called Emily and Anne.
As for the e-luv thing, blame my mum for that. She was always saying things like 'Ee, love, don't do that' and 'Ee, love, you look so cute I could eat you'.
I just assumed that was my name, and now it's what everyone in my family calls me. They're never going to let me forget it.
I am bored with writing. I have told you about my family, my job and my childhood. It is your turn.
e-luv

Sun 8.17 am

Dear e-luv,
Brontë? Oh, no. I bet this means you're looking for Darcy, like
everyone else on this bloody site.
Sinclair

 # Tue 6.42 pm

Sinclair!
Darcy? Fuck off. He was a miserable twat. And that book wasn't
written by any of the Brontës. Didn't they teach you anything at
school? It was Jane Austen. Now write to me properly.
e-luv

 # Tue 6.53 pm

I was beginning to like her. But despite the amusement I got from her e-mails, I had more pressing matters.

The cyberseduction of VOICE OF AN ANGLE. Not that I could imagine what kind of voice an angle would have.

I studied her ad for clues.

She liked to live life to the fullest. No surprises there.

She auditioned for Pop Idol, but didn't make the top twelve. She didn't actually say if she made the top 100 or even top 1000, but if it was judged on looks, she would have won.

She had the kind of face you just wanted to stare at. It had all the classic features: cute turned-up nose – check; big baby blue eyes – check; generous lips, even teeth – check; high, softly rounded cheekbones – check.

She also had some advice for whoever was reading her ad. 'Live your dreams,' she wrote, 'and don't dream your life.'

If I'd been playing the cliché game with Maya, that piece of philosophy would have been worth six points.

Wed 8.09 am

I decided that my best chance of success was to ignore her looks and focus on her personality. With a face like that, she must get comments all the time, so my theory was that she'd be so flattered someone had liked her for who she was that she would fall for me instantly.

I wrote:

> Hi, Voice of an Angle,
> I really liked your ad, especially what you said about living your dreams and not dreaming your life.
> I also loved that bit about dancing like no one was watching, loving like you've never been hurt before, and singing as though no one can hear you.
> Although I bet when you sing, everyone wants to hear you!
> Lord Brett

Her reply came back almost immediately:

> U sik perv! U R old enuf to be my dad!!!

I took this to mean she wasn't interested.

 # Wed 08.30 am

It's not hard to spot the older men in chatrooms, pretending to be twenty years younger than they really are so they can seduce the college chicks.

They get things spectacularly wrong, such as announcing how much they like the new CD by the *Limp Biscuits*.

I should know because I was that older man pretending to be twenty years younger than I really was.

 **Wed 10.16 am**

Princess Leia had summoned me to her chatroom. She had a problem and wanted my advice.

'Lord Brett, I've met someone.'

'That's great. Where did you meet? On the net?'

'Yes, in a Star Wars *forum*. There was a thread about whether or not Padmé ate fruit.'

'And does Padmé eat fruit?'

'No, of course not. So I got chatting to the guy who started the thread and we exchanged e-mails, talked on the phone, the usual.'

'And then you met up in real life?'

'Not exactly. He lives in Marin County, California.'

'Have you talked on the phone?'

'For around eight hours a night, sometimes more. Lord Brett, I really think I like him. How do you know if it's real?'

'I'm probably not the right person to ask that. What I learnt from the Lori disaster is that you have to have plenty in common. It's not enough to have an imagined physical attraction.'

'How long did it take you to realise it wasn't going to work out?'

'A few days, maybe. We both tried to force chemistry when there wasn't any.'

'Do you think I should fly over and meet him? Even if it doesn't work out, I've always wanted to vist the States. Plus, he's not far from George Lucas's ranch, and seeing that would be incredible. So what do you think? Should I risk it?'

I gave her the answer I knew she was desperate for me to give. It was the least I could do after everything she'd done for me.

'I think it's a great idea.'

Wed 12.12 pm

Before moving on to the lovely 2HOT4U, I decided to drop e-luv a line.

Dear e-luv,

I am relieved to hear that you harbour no feelings of affection towards Darcy.
I believe you were hinting that I should tell you a little more about myself.
My real name is Trevor. Which means we have something in common. Not that you're also called Trevor (that was a joke – apparently women like men with a GSOH), but that we were both named after someone famous.
My mum had an enormous crush on a 1940s actor called Trevor Howard.
I have no brothers or sisters and grew up in a small village outside Oxford.
Now your turn. What was your most embarrassing moment?
Mine was a tragic tale of humiliation involving full frontal nudity.
And on that cliffhanger, I'm going.

Sinclair

 # Wed 1.00 pm

I went to 2HOT4U's profile.

Her photo looked like something out of *Vogue*. She was astonishingly beautiful, and if I'd thought rationally, would have been unlikely to have been interested in a man who was ill, middle-aged, broke, overweight and divorced.

But that didn't occur to me as I read what she had to say about herself.

Greetings!!!
My name is Natalia. I very cheerful and cheerful girl! I want to have excellent (different) family, children. I the pensive and romantic girl. I kind and sympathetic. I like to communicate with people. At me it is a lot of

friends. I like to float, sunbathe. In the summer I leave on the nature. I like, when I lay on hot sand, and legs (foots) are in cool water. And having closed eyes you understand, that at present I am happy.
In general if I have interested you also you you want to continue with me the attitude (relation) write to me! I wait for your letter! I want to find fine the man which divided (shared) my pleasures and disappointments. I want to find you my dear. How to know, can we can sit together on a beach and enjoy the friend the friend and the nature! There can be you now read this letter.

Once again, I was in love.
Even though I didn't have a clue what she was on about.

Thu 8.53 am

There was no e-mail from e-luv.
This disappointed me more than I thought it would, so I wrote her a short note reminding her that it was her turn . I then composed my e-mail to 2HOT4U. It took nearly an hour to come up with this:

Dear Natalia,
I am the man who want to continue with you the attitude and share your pleasures and disappointments!
I am called Trevor and live in New Zealand. I am 40 years old.
Please tell me your hopes and dreams; your philosophy on life and what you look for in a man. Do you have any brothers or sisters?
I look forward to hearing from you
Trevor

Fri 7.31 am

I needn't have worried about e-luv. An e-mail was waiting for me the next morning.

Sinclair!
You seem to think that I've ever done something more embarrassing
than answering a personal ad.
You're right. I was 16 and the boy I was in love with, Nick Evans,
finally asked me out to a party. We sat in the dimly lit corner, me on his
lap, getting along really well. I reached over to the coffee table, grabbed
a handful of peanuts and put them in my mouth. After a few seconds,
I came to the hideous realisation that they weren't peanuts, they were
cigarette ends, and it wasn't a bowl, it was an ashtray. A violent
coughing fit was rapidly followed by me throwing up all over Nick.
Funnily enough, he never asked me out again.
What about you, Sinclair? Are there more embarrassing skeletons than
that in your closet?
e-luv

 Fri 8:17 am

Dear e-luv (or may I call you Charlotte?),
Not bad. But for sheer humiliation, try this.
Remember the Queen's Silver Jubilee? You're old enough, so you
bloody well should. Anyway, there were street parties everywhere,
including the market square of the small Oxfordshire town where I
lived. It was early on a summer's afternoon when some of my friends
at the pub bet me £10 that I wouldn't streak around the square. I
decided that it would be easy money. I went off to the toilet, got
undressed, ran out of the pub and towards the square. The first thing
I noticed was how crowded it was, but I reckoned it would take me
only a minute or so to complete the circuit. I took the first corner,
sprinted as fast as I could towards the second, which I tried to get
round a little too fast, twisted my ankle and went sprawling on to the
road. Stark bollock naked. I was in agony and people were starting to
form a circle around me to see if I was okay. There were several faces
I recognised. I tried to hobble back to the pub, where my clothes were,
but it was painfully slow and it seemed like half the population were
walking along with me, giggling and pointing.

Still, I did get the £10, so it wasn't a complete disaster. Now it's your turn. Tell me your biggest strength and your biggest weakness.
Sinclair

 Fri 11.35 am

One of the golden rules of Internet personals, as I soon discovered, was that if a woman was impossibly beautiful and her ad was impossible to understand, she was more than likely Russian. When I got my reply from 2HOT4U, I realised that she almost certainly belonged in that category.

She had apparently ignored my questions and instead listed her assets and requirements.

The thought crossed my mind that she hadn't even read my well thought-out e-mail, and that she sent this to all potential suitors.

She had this to say:

My dear love,
I am accurate, merry, easy-going, feminine, caring, intelligent, optimistic, sexual, serious about marriage, and also very neat person. My interests are car, cooking, going outdoors, travelling, dances, planting flowers.
I am searching for a man who would first of all love me and I will love him back. He should also be kind, caring, affectionate and loving children, older than me, over 40 years old.

I wondered if she was willing to rethink one or two of her demands, particularly the one about going out.

 Sun 8.04 am

Dear Sinclair (or may I call you Trevor?),
To answer your nosy questions.
My biggest strength? Immunity to gamma rays and the ability to deflect bullets with my bare hands.

Weakness? Answering your fucking stupid questions when I should know better.
Here's one for you. Do you have IM? If not, get it right now.
Charlotte

She was asking if I had Instant Messenger. This was a kind of intimate chatroom for two, where you type words into a panel, and the other person can see and respond.

Every spotty, socially awkward fifteen-year-old on the planet had it. And naturally, so did I.

 # Sun 4.41 pm

I had already had first-hand experience of a beautiful Russian goddess.

A few months ago, one came round to my house. She was in her late twenties, tall, slim and utterly, breathtakingly gorgeous.

The man with her was a middle-aged middle manager for an insurance company. He was at least six inches shorter than her, with an old-fashioned pudding-bowl haircut, much the same as the one I had when I was about ten. He wore the kind of glasses everyone wore when I was about twenty.

I vaguely knew him — he was an online friend of Leanne's, and was so unattractive that she hadn't even got engaged to him. His name was Mark. At least I was pretty sure it was.

'Hi, Trevor,' he announced, as though we were long lost pals. 'We were just passing, so I thought we'd drop in and say hello. This is Irina, by the way.'

I invited them in. Mark (I think) and Irina sat together on the sofa. He put his arm around her possessively, while she held his knee with the same enthusiasm she would have shown had she been clutching radioactive waste.

The body language wasn't looking good for Mark, or whatever his name was. He was obviously dragging her round to the homes of everyone he'd ever met, just to show her off.

'Irina's just arrived. She's moving over to be with me. We're in love,' he said, looking at her for confirmation, 'aren't we, darling?'

She looked at him and nodded robotically.

'We're just off to the beach,' he continued. 'Any excuse to see the lovely lady in a bikini.'

And then he *winked* at me.

I looked at Irina, hoping she would see the sympathy in my eyes, but her face remained expressionless. Later, I heard that she had decided to go back to Kiev. Apparently, the price of security and freedom was a little too high.

 ## Mon 9.27 pm

I was surprisingly nervous about my first IM session with Charlotte. It reminded me of the time I had to ring Maya, which was when I first realised I couldn't always hide behind pre-prepared quips or well-rehearsed throwaway comments.

Sometimes, I'd have to be spontaneous.

I was seeing plenty of similarities between Maya, my long lost love, and Charlotte, my new-found friend, apart from the fact that they both worked in bookshops.

Both were good company, and made me feel as though I was taking part in a conversation, not an interrogation. They were also smarter than the average chatroom user, which wasn't necessarily a good thing.

 ## Tue 1:12 pm

There's a website called Hot or Not, which is one of the main attractions of the Internet. It allows you to pass judgement on people's looks from the comfort of your own home.

It works like this. Someone puts their photo up and the rest of the world tells them how attractive or unattractive they are on a scale of one to ten, where one is truly hideous and ten is Pamela Anderson.

I spent days on end providing people with my opinions on their pictures. And then Charlotte made the mistake of mentioning in passing that

I looked pretty good for my age. When I put that together with Jacqui's comment about me not being bad-looking, I felt it was time to give my ego a major boost and put the Alan Rickman photo up on hotornot.com.

First, I checked out the competition.

A lot of the men seemed to have misplaced their shirts when the pictures were being taken. They also seemed to spend an alarming amount of time at the gym.

The hard work appeared to have paid off, with many of them scoring marks in the 7.5–9.5 range.

My photo went up at 9.10 on Saturday morning. By lunchtime more than 350 women had already checked me out, and my score was a very respectable 7.1.

I was feeling pretty good about myself, and wasn't even worried when I logged on that night and saw that just under 1000 had given their verdicts and the average had gone down to 6.4.

The next day I was feeling a little less good, as my score appeared to be in freefall. It seemed that the more people voted, the more your score went down. By teatime I was at 5.6.

The tactic of voting for myself over and over failed to stem the tide, and by the end of the week I had finally stabilised.

The only problem was that I was now down to 4.9.

I quietly removed my picture from the site and went back to judging others.

 **Wed 8.08 am**

There was a postcard that morning with a picture of lots of trees and rolling green hills. I looked on the back, where it said simply:

This is the best thing that ever happened to me and I'm so glad I listened to you.
Love
Alice
xxx

Alice? I didn't know any Alice. And then I noticed the postmark, which said Marin County, California, and I immediately knew that Alice was Princess Leia's real name.

 # Wed 5.12 pm

As I sat at the computer preparing notes for the Charlotte chat, I had an epiphany.

I suddenly realised what was missing in my life. There was a huge, yawning gap caused by my self-enforced chatroom abstinence.

But I knew deep inside that I was merely postponing the inevitable return. The whole excursion into personal ads had been a fiasco. All I'd got from it was one woman who took exception to my age, another whose age I took exception to, and one who spoke in a language of her own invention.

I knew what I had to do.

I had to go back to where I truly belonged. The Paris Chatroom.

 # Wed 5.59 pm

As soon as I logged on, I felt a strange calmness descend over me. It felt like I had arrived home after a lengthy absence and had just stepped through the front door.

Everywhere I looked, I saw comforting reminders of the way things were. The LOLs, ROTFLs and the smiley icons.

There were the familiar questions and requests:

'*Where are you from?*', '*Anyone wanna chat?*' and '*17m wants phone sex*'.

I took in the attention-seeking behaviour of HORNY2NITE, as he posted a message simply reading 'HORNY2NITE attempts a magic spell and explodes in a ball of fire'.

I saw people posting random lyrics, for reasons that weren't entirely clear.

I saw that lovers still liked to do the same things, such as long walks, road trips and getting drunk.

I even saw a few familiar names. And one in particular caught my eye. Lady Gwinnivear.

🧑 Wed 6.10 pm

She was the first to break the cybersilence.

'M'lord. I am glowing with happiness. Yet I am not surprised to see you. I knew thou wouldst be back for me.'

'M'lady, the last I heard, you had found a Scotsman. How's it going with him?'

'That loser? He turned out to be no gentleman, unlike you, m'lord. You know, I still play that tape you sent me, every night.'

Why would she do that? It was horrible, from what I remembered. Designed to let her know how cool I was. She wasn't meant to actually listen to it.

'So, m'lady. Did you really know I'd be back?'

'Of course. The cosmos is more powerful than thou realises. I asked my psychic if I would see you again and she told me you were my destiny.'

By this time, every rational fibre in my body was screaming out for me to leave. But I couldn't. I watched helplessly as my fingers followed a predictable and well-worn path across the keyboard.

'May I enquire as to what thou art wearing?'

'LOL. I didn't need a psychic to tell me that was coming, did I?'

'No, m'lady.'

'I'm wearing an old pair of jeans, pink blouse and the tiniest little red thong you ever did see. You'd like it.'

'Can I ask you a favour?'

'You want me to send it to you?'

'If you wouldn't mind.'

'Sure, m'lord. Anything else you want me to send? I got some new pics done.'

'I'd love to see them. I'm still at the same address.'

'Oh, I know that, m'lord. Hey, one more thing – do you have any pets?'

'I don't – why?'

'Would you like one? I guess I'm saying that if you had a real cute pet, *would you look after it and feed it and stuff?'*

'Of course, m'lady.'

I didn't really know where she was going with this, but I did know that women liked men to be fond of animals. She then said something that was really, worryingly eccentric, even by Jacqui's standards.

'Well, I'm glad, because I found the cutest pet for you. I'll mail it with the pics and panties.'

And with that, she was gone. I sat back in my chair. In front of me chatroom life was going on as normal. People were arguing over which songs were better, they were trying to persuade each other to cyber, and they were arranging to meet up again the following day.

Walking away from the computer that night was even harder than usual.

 Thu 8.31 am

'Sinclair! Where the fuck are you, you fat old twat?'

That onscreen message was waiting for me the next morning as soon as I logged on to IM for my 9 am meeting with Charlotte.

It seemed that she had arrived a few minutes early and was getting impatient.

'Hurry up. I'm not in the best of moods.'

I typed as fast as I could, eager not to make things worse.

'I'm here. So what's the cause of this departure from your normal cheery state of mind?'

'A fucking customer. Do you know what she said to me?'

'No.'

'She said I reminded her of Caroline fucking Quentin. Can you fucking believe that?'

'Well, you do look like her.'

That's what I typed. But then cowardice got the better of me before I could press Send, so I deleted it and wrote an alternate version.

'But you're much better looking. And younger.'

'Good choice of words, Sinclair. There is hope for you yet. I bet no one's ever mistaken you for anyone famous.'

'Well, actually a few people have noticed a resemblance to Alan Rickman.'

'Alan Rickman? Oh, Sinclair, you have just made my day. If it wasn't such an annoying thing to do, I would type something like ROTFL.'
We had more in common than I thought.

 ## Fri 2.19 pm

Jacqui and I, on the other hand, had even less in common than I thought. But she still excited me.

It was easy to put up with the bizarre olde worlde English and constant per ses because she gave me the one thing I craved almost above all else. An endless supply of underwear.

Red thongs, white silk French knickers, Italian lace, run-of-the-mill cotton panties... They were arriving in the mail at the rate of two or three a week.

For the first time, I felt I had found a woman who truly understood me.

I'd been wondering how we could take our relationship to the next level. She provided me with the solution in our very next chat.

 ## Fri 5.18 pm

'M'lord, dost thou have a webcam?'
I was willing to bet that not one person in medieval times had ever spoken that sentence.

But the concept was so brilliant, so perfectly in tune with my cyber needs that I couldn't believe I hadn't thought of it before.

It also meant that she had a webcam. This gorgeous, young, exotic dancer had a webcam.

I finally discovered what the phrase 'giddy with excitement' meant. At last, I would be able to see her go through her repertoire of exotic dances.

And even though I wasn't yet sure what form of sexual activity would now be possible, I was pretty sure it would be better than cybersex.

'M'lady, I anticipate taking delivery of a webcam at my castle within the next three days.'

 **Fri 7.54 pm**

After placing an online order for a webcam, including express delivery, I met up with Charlotte on IM.

She seemed in a better frame of mind than the last time we'd spoken.

'Sinclair, I wish to know about your tastes in furniture. Look around you and describe what you see.'

I looked around and saw a few tatty chairs and plenty of cardboard boxes.

'Minimalist. Now it's your turn. Name your favourite Jerry Springer *episode.'*

'Close one. It's between I Want to Marry My Brother *and* 600 Pound Angry Mom. *Over to you for worst fashion mistake.'*

'That'd be wrestling boots. I was convinced they were going to catch on, so I wore them for about six months. Never saw anyone else in them, so I stopped. Most annoying boy band?'

'N'Sync. Blue. A1. All of them. Especially when they do that fucking stupid bowed head thing before they start singing. What poster was on your wall when you were a kid?'

'The one for Rocky 4, *where he beat Ivan Drago and avenged Apollo Creed. What's the one food you would live on if you were only allowed to live on one food?'*

'Potato salad. Most stupid Olympic sport?'

'Showjumping. If you had to shag either Fred Elliot, Mike Baldwin or Ken Barlow from Coronation Street, *who would you choose?'*

'Mike Baldwin. Worst film?'

'Random Hearts.'

'Hey, my Auntie Mary gave me the DVD of that for Christmas.'

'Did it come with any extras? Like a plot, maybe?'

'Very droll, Sinclair. If you were better looking, I might find you intriguing.'

I was about to say the same thing. But I didn't.

Tue 8.50 am

I held the package from Jacqui to my ear, just to make sure she hadn't really tried to send me a puppy through the post, but I needn't have worried.

When I opened it, there amongst the photos and underwear was a small box with a picture of an egg-shaped plastic toy. In its centre was a small digital screen. The words right next to it said:

Tamagotchi is a tiny pet from cyberspace who needs your love to survive and grow. If you take care of your Tamagotchi pet, it will slowly grow bigger and healthier and more beautiful every day. But if you neglect your little cyber creature, your Tamagotchi may grow up to be mean or ugly. How old will your Tamagotchi be when it returns to its home planet? What kind of virtual caretaker will you be?

So this was my new pet. According to the handwritten note from Jacqui, I was to call him Lancelot.

I pressed a couple of buttons and a pulsing egg appeared. A short while later, Lancelot had been hatched and was demanding food.

I fed him. But apparently this wasn't enough to make him happy. He wanted me to play with him.

I'd had enough already. I put Lancelot into a drawer so he could get some sleep. Whether he needed it or not.

Tue 2.32 pm

'Hey Trevor bet you cant guess who this is. Ill give you a clue. Im a girl.'

I had no idea. All I knew was that she called herself Sunflower, I hadn't seen her in Paris Chat before and that she sounded like an eight-year-old.

The reason for this became clear when she revealed her identity. She was an eight-year-old.

Cheyenne.

I hadn't heard from her or Lori since they left in the middle of the night, following the dinner party disaster.

'Hey Cheyenne, it's great to hear from you. What have you been up to?'

'Just school and stuff.'

'So you're back in the States?'

'Yea were living with granny and granpa.'

'And have you seen your dad since you got back?'

'Just once. We went to give him his TV back. He said that he wasnt going to make me go and live with him.'

I suspected the return of the TV might be his price for dropping the custody threats, but I didn't want to shatter any illusions.

'And how's your mom?'

What I really wanted to ask was 'Has she found anyone, and if she has, what's he got that I haven't got, and anyway, why didn't she fancy me?' but this didn't seem either the time or place for such questions.

'Moms good. She says as soon as she finds a job were gonna move out of here and get a place of our own.'

'What kind of work is she looking for?'

'Any old thing. She says shell even wash dishes if she has to.'

For the second time in as many months, I felt a sudden and overwhelming need to make a grand, sweeping gesture to Lori – although this time there was a clearer motivation.

Guilt.

After Cheyenne left, I went to the cupboard under the stairs and removed a hand-carved Maori mask, a Wanganui and District telephone directory from 1932, and several other items.

I then spent the next thirty minutes putting them all up on eBay. It was well worth it. A week later, they'd sold for a total of $1335, which I deposited into Lori's account.

 Wed 3.36 pm

I was peering into the bathroom mirror, preparing for my webcam debut. I'd been practising holding my stomach in for long periods on end, and now I was applying a few cosmetic touches. Specifically, a fake tan on my face.

I didn't dare risk Jacqui seeing me in my normal pallid state, and followed the instructions to the letter, including exfoliating and thoroughly rubbing in the tanning cream to avoid streaking.

When I had finished I stepped back to admire my work. It looked good. And, more importantly, it looked convincing.

I was ready.

 ## Wed 4.44 pm

I sat down at the computer, positioned the webcam and placed my sheets of ad libs and amusing throwaway lines just out of its range.

We were due to meet in about a minute, which gave me just enough time to put some music on – music I knew she liked. My unlistenable punk. Designed to let her know how cool I was.

I wore a sweatshirt with the cover of *The Great Gatsby* printed on it. Designed to let her know how intelligent I was.

And my face looked tanned. Designed to let her know what a healthy lifestyle I led.

Suddenly, the window on the screen flickered into life.

I could now make out a woman who bore a passing resemblance to the divine creature whose glamour shot had pride of place on my bedside table.

She was a plumper, older, less glamorous version.

Her blonde hair was tied back, her lipstick was bright red and she wore a pale blue camisole.

She was leaning forward and squinting, with a puzzled look on her face.

'Hi,' she said, '*I'm looking for Trevor. Calls himself Lord Brett. Is he around?*'

It crossed my mind that maybe this was the downside to sending old and misleading photos. When you did finally come face to face, even if you were continents apart, you were impossible to recognise.

'*Tis I, m'lady, Lord Brett in person. How art thou?*'

Was that a sliver of disappointment I saw crossing her face? No, it was a fucking great cloud of disappointment.

'*Lord Brett? Oh, okay. I thought maybe you were, like, your dad, if you know what I mean.*'

'*If I may say, m'lady, thou art looking more beautiful than your pictures ever suggested. I am truly honoured.*'

She ignored me and her voice took on a belligerent edge.

'*Those pics you sent. When did you say they were taken?*'

'*Oh, them? I dunno. A couple of years ago. Maybe three or four.*'

'*How's about ten or fifteen?*'

I nodded in agreement.

'*Yeah, that sounds about right.*'

I noticed that when she became confrontational, she stopped using thees and thous. I also pondered the wisdom of pointing out that her photos were hardly an accurate representation, but wisely decided against it.

She stared at the camera, as though trying to make up her mind about something.

Eventually, and much to my relief, she broke the silence.

'*Why couldn't you send a more recent photo? Y'know, you're really not that bad-looking.*'

'*Why thank you, m'lady.*'

She smiled, and looked straight at me.

'*You got a pack of playing cards there, m'lord?*'

'*Yeah, I think so. Why?*'

'*Go get 'em. Me and thee, we're gonna play strip poker.*'

 Wed 4.57 pm

I literally ran around the flat looking for cards. I pulled drawers out and flung cupboards open, scattering the contents, searching frantically.

I found what I was looking for in my bedside drawer. I'd put them there when Kate had come down. For some reason, I thought she might like to see some of the card tricks I'd taught myself when there was nothing better to do.

Right now, I had something a lot better to do.

 **Wed 5.05 pm**

I sat back down and readied myself as she explained the rules.

We were both to shuffle our packs in full view and then deal ourselves two cards, face down. Then one of us (we'd take it in turns) would deal another three 'communal' cards face up in full view.

Whoever had the best hand would win, and the other person would have to remove an article of clothing.

There was no time to waste.

This was the moment my whole life had been building towards.

I dealt myself a queen and a four.

She dealt herself two cards, then laid out a nine, a jack – and a queen! Giving me a pair.

It wasn't enough. She had a straight.

I removed my sweatshirt to reveal my *Ponch from CHiPS* T-shirt. Her expression changed from smugness to confusion. Perhaps she wasn't a *CHiPS* fan.

'*M'lord? Maybe it's the camera, but it looks like your arms are white and your face and neck are kinda orange.*'

I mumbled something about forgetting to put sunblock on my face, but I don't think she believed me.

The next hand went my way, and off came her camisole to reveal a white bra.

I won the next one, too.

She stood up, slowly unzipped her tartan skirt and it fell to the floor, leaving her standing in a small pair of very brief matching tartan knickers

'*Like what you see, m'lord? I got them in bonnie Scotland.*'

'*Most acceptable, m'lady.*'

'*Well, don't just stare. Deal some cards.*'

And that was the start of my losing streak.

My jack high was beaten by a pair of twos.

My full house lost out to a flush.

My pair of tens weren't enough against her pair of kings.

Which was why I was sitting on my chair in front of the computer totally naked, except for a thick coating of instant tan on my face and neck.

And that was the exact moment that Jacqui suddenly remembered she had to go to work.

 # Thu 7.59 pm

Charlotte asked me if I'd ever met up with any women in real life that I'd met over the Internet, so I told her about my experiences with Kate and Lori. She surprised me by admitting that she had recently met up with a couple of men who had replied to her ad.

The last time was a bit of a disaster.

The arty sounding chap in his thirties had turned out to have an unpleasant ponytail/goatee combination and his job was printing wallpaper. He obviously liked it because during the meal, he insisted on explaining in excruciating detail the press techniques involved in producing the restaurant's wallpaper.

She didn't stay for dessert.

I then discovered why she'd brought up the subject.

She said that she had to cut our chat short because she was due to meet someone called Spider, whose reply was a cut above the others. He'd described himself as a writer and a big John Waters fan. His photo looked okay, too, so she had agreed to meet up on neutral territory.

I said that I hoped it went well for her, but the truth was, I was hoping it didn't.

For some strange reason, which I didn't yet understand, I felt a twinge of jealousy.

 # Fri 2.22 am

When you're in a chatroom, you never know what you're going to get. There was a perfect demonstration of this when I found myself in the Paris at one that morning, and found two chatters with similar-sounding names: Inyrdreams and Sweetdreamer (f24).

They couldn't have been more different.

This was my entire conversation with Inyrdreams.

'I say! Would anyone care to chat to Lord Brett Sinclair?'

'So, Lord Brett – you a real English lord or what?'

'Alas, Inyrdreams, I am not. Lord Brett was a character in a hopeless 1970s TV show. The name is meant to be ironic.'

'Like rain on your wedding day?'

'More like a free ride when you've already paid. And is Inyrdreams your real name?'

'Yes.'

'Where are you from?'

'Newark, New Jersey. I bet you're going to ask me what I look like next.'

'What do you look like?'

'I'm 5' 5", 124 pounds, auburn hair cut short. I'm 23 and a Scorpio. Work as a paralegal for a smallish law firm. Anything else?'

'No, that's probably all I'll need to fall in love with you. Will you marry me?'

'Nope. Any more questions?'

'Have you ever considered the herbal approach to maximum fitness?'

'Hey, I tried selling that shit to help me through school. I've still got the boxes in my basement.'

'The only reason you failed was because you stopped trying.'

'No, it wasn't. It was because the product was basically overpriced crap.'

And this was my chat with Sweetdreamer (f24).

'Hi, Sweetdreamer. Care to chat with Lord Brett?'

'K.'

'Bet you thought I was a real English lord.'

'No.'

'Alas, Sweetdreamer (f24), you were right. I am not. Lord Brett was a character in a hopeless 70s TV show. The name is meant to be ironic.'

'Huh?'

'You know. Like rain on your wedding day?'

'Huh?'

'It's that Alanis Morrisette song, Ironic. You know the one?'

'Dont like Alanis.'

'*Where are you from?*'
'*Canada.*'
'*What do you look like?*'
'*Im rubinesk.*'
'*Will you marry me?*'
'*Whatever.*'
'*Have you ever considered the herbal approach to maximum fitness?*'
'*Gotta go.*'
The only thing Inyrdreams and Sweetdreamer (f24) had in common was a refusal to give me their e-mail addresses.

 # Fri 7.44 pm

I was having an IM chat with Charlotte, trying to find a way to casually ask how her date with Spider had gone. In the end I just came out with it.
'*Back to the drawing board, Sinclair,*' she typed. '*He was a scrawny little fucker who took himself way too seriously.*'
I smiled with relief and then found myself asking her something I really shouldn't have been asking.
'*So what are you wearing?*'
If she found the question a little odd, she didn't let on. Maybe, like so many other women on the Internet, she'd heard it so many times that she'd become immune.
'*Wool cableknit sweater with a snowflake pattern, overalls, thermal underwear and hiking boots.*'
'*That's not true, is it?*'
'*No, Sinclair, it's not. Now isn't this where you ask me my deepest sexual fantasy?*'
'*What's your deepest sexual fantasy?*'
'*Not telling you. What's yours?*'
'*To have sex with a woman again some time before I die.*'
'*How about something more realistic?*'
I sensed that her perception of how attractive I was differed from mine.

 Mon 4.57 pm

'*So, how's Lancelot?*' asked Jacqui in one of our increasingly frequent webcam chats. '*Can I see him?*'

Shit. I'd forgotten all about Lancelot since shoving him away in a drawer minutes after he arrived.

'*Umm...I'd rather not. Thing is, he's asleep and I don't want to wake him.*'

'*Hey, I understand. Is he growing?*'

'*Real fast. He's getting so big, you wouldn't recognise him.*'

'*And you don't mind getting up in the night to feed him?*'

'*Not at all.*'

'*And how about changing diapers?*'

'*Hey, I enjoy it.*'

'*Do you like playing with him?*'

I suddenly realised that we weren't really talking about a Tamagotchi any more.

She was trying to find out what sort of a dad I'd make.

Wed 1.12 pm

I was a man on a mission: to turn myself into the best poker player I could possibly be.

The frustration of being fully naked while Jacqui was still in her underwear had spurred me on to reach for new heights. Next time we played, I wanted to win. I hadn't even seen her tits yet.

So I went online, and on the countless poker websites I found page after page of invaluable tips, which I faithfully copied down into my notebook. Even when I had no idea what they meant, such as this: 'In Texas Hold'em, you can bet with an ace or two minor over cards on the flop, but you should fold if someone raises your bet.'

I was sure that would come in useful some day.

What I did understand was the importance of watching my opponent's habits and not trying to beat the other players, but to let them try to beat me.

It was also apparently helpful to choose less skilful people to play against, although I suspected that Jacqui had already discovered that one.

I even learnt from another source that it was important to know when to hold 'em and when to fold 'em. And that you should never count your money when you're sitting at the table.

Tue 9.36 am

When I got back from the supermarket, there was another package waiting for me. It was from Jacqui, which gave me a fair idea of what was inside.

I wasn't disappointed.

I took out a pair of very brief tartan panties. As I was about to throw away the envelope, I noticed there was a note inside. It said:

M'Lord,
I figured you'd need all the help you can get. So here's one less thing I'll be wearing next time we play poker.
Lady Gwinnivear xxxx

Tue 3.24 pm

The one person everyone in the chatroom was desperate to avoid was Sam Malone.

Named after the charismatic barman on *Cheers*, our Sam was the exact opposite. He was the most boring person I had ever met – and once you got trapped with him, there was no way out.

'*Hi, how's it going?*' was his usual opening gambit, followed by '*So, do you think Ross and Rachel are going to get together?*'

Maya had once, in a moment of weakness, given him her phone number when he told her he was going to be spending a few weeks in Vermont. He ended up staying with her for the entire time. She described every minute in his company as feeling like an hour with anyone else, and got increasingly angry as he ate her food, drank her drink and used up the hot water without offering a cent towards his stay.

When he finally went home, he'd ring her once or twice a day. As far as I knew, he still did.

Most people had strategies to avoid being stuck with Sam Malone. Some would pretend to be in a private conversation with someone else. Others would quit the room and re-enter under a different name. I thought this was a rude and underhand thing to do, so I always talked to him.

We were having a chat a couple of nights ago.

For once he didn't want to talk about plot developments on *Friends*. He wanted to talk about his forthcoming trip to Australia and New Zealand.

He asked for my address and phone number, so we could meet up when he got to Wellington.

I promptly quit the room and re-entered under a different name.

 ## Tue 5.23 pm

I tentatively opened the kitchen drawer, knowing that it would probably contain bad news.

Lifting Lancelot out, my worst fears were confirmed.

At precisely 2.31.24 the previous Wednesday, he had expired.

I felt awful. Close to tears. I tried telling myself that it was just a piece of plastic with a computer chip inside, but that didn't make any difference.

I wished I could turn back time.

 ## Tue 7.28 pm

We were sitting around a green baize cyber poker table, Slickrick, Cloudancer4, Hoppingsnake, Snowman and I.

I had bought $100 worth of chips on my credit card and was ready to play online poker for the first time.

As soon as I saw the speed of the game, I began to panic. Everything was moving way too fast. These people had played before. It was important to give the impression that I had as well.

I was dealt a six of hearts and a king of diamonds.

Slickrick called $5. So did Cloudancer4.

Then it was my turn. A clock appeared onscreen, counting down. I had five seconds to decide what to do.

So I just did what everyone else was doing and called $5.

That's when it all started getting out of hand. Snowman raised to $10. Hoppingsnake followed suit, and Slickrick raised to $20.

Without really knowing what I was doing, I raised to $30. I think I was hoping to frighten everyone off with an outrageous bluff.

It didn't work.

Within about a minute, there was a king of spades, a ten of hearts and a three of clubs on the table.

I had nothing. Not even a pair.

I folded. I'd bet all my money on a totally useless hand.

Which meant I'd lost every cent of my $100 in just under a minute. And Slickrick had won $255 with two pairs, eights and sevens.

It was easy money. If you knew what you were doing.

 Wed 4.13 pm

I was chatting with BettyBoop33, when she asked me the question that anyone who spends any length of time in chatrooms will inevitably be asked.

'If you could have a dinner party with five people, living or dead, who would you choose?'

I went through the options in my mind.

Pamela Anderson, definitely.

Britney Spears, yes. As long as she was wearing the school uniform she wore in the *Hit Me Baby* video.

I'd also have to have one of the *Spice Girls* – either Posh or Baby. Probably Posh.

Then it gets difficult. How are you meant to choose between Debbie Harry (late '70s version), Kim Wilde (early '80s), and Catherine Zeta-Jones (mid '90s)?

And how can you leave out Farrah Fawcett from the *Charlie's Angels* days?

In the end I got it down to Pamela, Britney, Debbie, Posh and Farrah.

Of course, I kept these thoughts to myself, and gave the same answer I – and everyone else – gives when asked the question.

'I'd invite Mother Teresa, Gandhi, Nelson Mandela, William Shakespeare and Martin Luther King.'

 Thu 8.12 pm

'Who's your favourite Pokemon?'

Charlotte was never one for easy questions, and this required serious consideration.

'I'm going to say Jigglypuff,' I said finally. *'I like the way he sends everyone to sleep, and he doesn't lose anything when he evolves into Wigglystuff.'*

'Wigglytuff.'

'How did you know that?'

'My kids like him.'

Kids? It was the first I'd heard about this. She'd never mentioned them before.

'So how many do you have?'

'Kids? Three. Ben's fifteen, Paul's fourteen and Sophie's twelve. What about you? Any mini Sinclairs wandering around causing chaos and destruction?'

'No, wasn't married long enough to carry on the family line. Anything else you want to know?'

'Yes. What's the worst lyric you've ever heard?'

'Take that look from off your face. Oasis. Forgot what the song was called. If you had fifteen minutes to live, what would you do?'

'Probably kill myself. Favourite story of rock star behaviour?'

'The bloke from the Go Betweens, *who decided to dye his hair grey so he could look like Blake Carrington out of* Dynasty. *Ever stolen anything from a shop?'*

'When I was eleven, I tried to steal a 10-foot fishing rod from a local department store. Somehow, one of the salesmen noticed me trying to sneak out with it. Greatest invention of the 20th century?'

'Call waiting. Last time you asked someone for an autograph?'

'I wish you hadn't asked me that. It was Jeffrey fucking Archer. He did a signing at the shop.'

'Hey, doesn't he have the power to send everyone to sleep, too?'

'Indeed he does. But enough frivolity. You can fuck off now, Sinclair. It's time to make the kids' breakfast.'

'Say hello to them from me.'

After she'd gone I found myself at a loose end. But not for long. The lure of online poker was becoming impossible to resist.

Tue 3.48 pm

I decided that if I was to get credibility with my poker peers, I'd need a new name. Lord Brett Sinclair just didn't cut it, especially among the likes of Maverick, AnnieO and TinyTexan.

I needed a name to reflect my authority and to strike fear into the hearts of my opponents. It had to make a statement.

From now on, I would be known as Pokeman.

Tue 7.55 pm

Before logging on to the poker site, I decided to take a walk and clear my head. It was a warm night and I was wearing just my authentic Ferd Perry shirt and a pair of shorts. I felt good, so decided to walk to the very limit of my comfort zone – the minimart, which was around 800 yards away. I'd only managed that once before, and it took every ounce of courage I could summon.

I passed the dentist and got on to the main road, waiting for the familiar feeling of helplessness and anxiety to come.

But it never arrived. Even when I could see the supermarket. And even when I walked straight past it without a backward glance.

I kept going into uncharted territory, seeing things I remembered from the distant past and things I'd never seen before. There was the library, which had had a whole new wing added. A cluster of fast food outlets had sprung out of nowhere, lined up alongside each other where the fire station once stood. Whole buildings had been knocked down and replaced with a sprawling 'retirement village'.

It was then that I realised how much life had already passed me by while I had been stuck at home.

And it was equally clear that there was a whole world waiting for me outside my tiny little suburb.

Chapter 8

 Fri 5.23 pm

I scanned the list of chatters and my pulse quickened when I saw that Lady Gwinnivear was there. I quickly fired off a private message to her.

'M'lady, may I ask how thoust day has been?'

'Greetings, kind sir. It has been real good. Did you get my package?'

'Indeed I did, m'lady. So now I know what you're not wearing, how about you tell me what you are wearing?'

Before she had time to answer, a cyberfight broke out in the room. Sk8erboy and Tetris (f16) had been having a heated discussion, and Sk8erboy had just told her to piss off.

And this was when Tetris (f16)'s cyberboyfriend, Brainiac, joined in.

'Dude, you betta say yr sorry to the lady or I'll whip your ass.'

'Yeah? Come on then. Bring it on.'

Tetris (f16) tried to intervene.

'Come on, babe,' she typed. 'Leave it. He ain't worth it.'

But Brainiac was determined to defend his woman's honour. I could imagine him hunched angrily over his keyboard, rapidly jabbing away at the letters.

'You got 5 seconds to apologise, muthafucker. One... two... three... four... five.'

'Fuck you,' said Sk8erboy from the safety of his bedroom.

Tetris (f16) was still trying to play the peacemaker.

'Babe, just walk away. He's nothing.'

But Brainiac was having none of it.

'Dude, I'm gonna track you down and when I find you, I'm gonna punch yr fuckin lights out.'

'Yeah? You are so going down, man. I'll rip your head off.'

It appeared that all this teenage testosterone flooding the chatroom had touched Jacqui in some primeval way.

'M'lord, let's have a webcam meeting tomorrow at 7 your time,' she whispered. *'And don't forget to bring a pack of cards.'*

 # Wed 3.06 am

Cards were the reason I had dragged myself out of bed at 3 am. I hadn't been able to sleep, such was the excitement of putting my new-found poker skills into practice.

I logged in under my new name of Pokeman, bought $1000 of chips on my credit card and sat down to play.

There were only two others at the table. Slickrick, who always seemed to be sitting at the same table, and Firefighter, who I'd never seen before.

I had come up with a strategy that seemed to make perfect sense at three in the morning.

I would wait for a good hand, then bet the lot on it.

It was bold and it was reckless.

Just as I was wondering if it was ever going to happen, I was dealt two aces, which is about as good as you can get. I raised my opponents $200.

My unchanging poker face was unnecessary, considering neither of them could see me, but it was good practice for my game with Jacqui later on in the morning. Firefighter couldn't take the heat and folded, but Slickrick stayed in the game, even when I raised him $400 after seeing a pair of kings appear on the table, giving me two pairs.

We both stayed in the final round of betting, putting in another $400 each. I soon find out why he hadn't dropped out. His full house was enough to win and I was $1000 down.

Yet for reasons that will become clear later, I didn't mind at all.

Thu 10.02 am

I'd gone to pick up some mineral pills at the local healthfood shop, which I'd been taking for a while and felt as though they might be doing a bit of good in terms of slightly increased energy.

They shop had run out, but the assistant recommended colloidal minerals, which were the same thing in liquid form.

They sounded familiar, and when I got home I realised why.

In the cupboard under the stairs I found a box containing twenty-four bottles of the stuff – part of my unsold Herbal Solutions stock.

I started taking it and weeks later, when I felt how much good it was doing me, I wondered whether things really might happen for a reason.

 # Tue 4:01 pm

I was sitting at the computer in a state of nervous excitement. The minutes had been slowly ticking away all day and now I was just an hour away from the long-awaited strip poker rematch with Jacqui.

Much of the afternoon had been spent trying to decide what to wear. I was torn between:

1. Giving in to my ill-advised exhibitionist impulses and having just a T-shirt and shorts, or
2. Concealing my ageing body by wearing far more layers of clothing than someone would normally wear on a warm summer's day.

In the end, common sense prevailed, and I had on three T-shirts, sweatshirt, coat, jeans, boxers, socks and knee bandage.

I was hoping this last item would qualify as clothing, but would understand if she disagreed. When Jacqui walked towards her camera, I couldn't help but smile. She was wearing the same skirt as last time, the only difference being that this time I knew she had nothing on underneath.

I recognised her top because I'd sent it to her. It was a white T-shirt, with a circular yellow and black design. Inside the circle was the number 700, which was surrounded by the words *Battle of Stirling Bridge 1297–1997*.

I'd got this for her from Macbraveheart.co.uk, together with a limited edition poster that read, *Everything I know about life, I learnt from Braveheart*.

The T-shirt wasn't a very nice design, but that didn't matter. It would be coming off soon enough.

After exchanging greetings, we got straight down to business.

I dealt myself a pair of twos. It was going to be my day. This was confirmed when there was another two on the table, giving me three of a kind.

That warm, optimistic feeling lasted all of a minute, which was how long it took Jacqui to proudly announce she had a full house, and for me to remove my coat.

The next hand was slightly different, in that I knew I'd lose as soon as I saw my cards. She'd got a flush, but didn't need it. All I had was a king high.

The pattern continued. The one bright spot was my spectacular win on the fifth hand of the day, when my three aces were more than a match for her lowly pair, and off came her shoes.

Apart from that, I was losing badly. I was down to one shirt, one pair of jeans and one pair of boxers.

This wasn't going to plan. The thought that she might somehow be cheating crossed my mind, but I couldn't see how.

I watched her closely next time she dealt, but it all looked above board.

Still – was it really possible within the laws of chance for me to lose nine hands in a row? This was the thought running through my head as I reluctantly stepped out of my boxers following yet another humiliating loss.

I quickly sat down in the chair fully naked and adopted a bizarre position, my legs spread at right angles, which made it look as though I was thrusting my knob towards the camera in the manner of a 1970s heavy metal frontman.

I wasn't. I was just trying to make sure she couldn't see the huge red rashes that had recently reappeared on my outer thighs.

 Wed 10.15 pm

I was getting worried about Charlotte.

It had been nearly three days since I had heard from her, despite sending a flurry of e-mails and sitting by the computer, waiting for her to log on to IM.

Finally, I decided to try and track down her phone number so I could call and see if she was okay.

Using Google, I found out that the Brontë family had lived in a small village called Haworth in West Yorkshire. I then did a search of bookshops there that had websites. This yielded just two results.

The first made me fall in love at first sight. The pictures showed a proper old-fashioned bookshop that boasted it stocked 'everything from bestsellers to antiquarian prints'.

The shelves were roomy and uncluttered, and there were padded armchairs so people could sit and read at leisure.

But what really caught my eye was the last picture. In it, standing patiently behind the counter, was Charlotte.

I had found her.

 Wed 10.23 pm

'Hello, could I speak to Charlotte, please?'

'This is she. How can I help you?'

'Umm…it's Sinclair…you know, Trevor. In New Zealand. It was just that I haven't heard from you in a few days and I was wondering if you were okay.'

'Sinclair! Fucking hell. Actually the Internet has been down and they can't come and fix it until Monday. How the fuck did you get my number?'

This was the awkward part. There's a thin line between doing what I had done and stalking.

'I looked up the shop's website. It looks really nice.'

Luckily, she was in a rare good mood and didn't seem to mind.

'It's beautiful here, Sinclair. Wouldn't change it for the world.'

'What do you like most about it?'

'The pace of life. The fact it's a great place to bring up kids. The scenery… Do you like walking, Sinclair?'

'To tell you the truth…'

Now, when someone starts a sentence like that, they're about to lie. But not me. Not this time.

'To tell you the truth, I get panic attacks when I go out, so I tend to stay indoors.'

There. I'd said it.

'That's sad.'

'But I do think I'm getting better, slowly but surely. Especially the last couple of weeks.'

'You must tell me all about it when my computer's up and running again. I'd better get back to work now, Sinclair. I have a customer waiting, but thanks for your concern.'

'That's okay.'

'One more thing – I meant to tell you. I won't be online for a couple of weeks in early November. I'm going away for a booksellers' conference.'

'Somewhere exciting?'

'You tell me, Sinclair. It's in your part of the world. Sydney.'

 Sat 3.40 pm

There was an e-mail from Jacqui. It said to meet her in the chatroom as soon as possible because she had some exciting news to share.

Hoping that this news was underwear-related, I got there as quickly as possible. She was waiting for me.

'M'lord, you'll never guess what?'

'Do tell, m'lady.'

'I will. But first I need to know if you believe in astrology. You don't have to believe in it per se, *just have an open mind about what I'm going to tell you.'*

This was intriguing, although I was disappointed that the conversation didn't seem to be heading in an erotic direction.

I toyed with the idea of replying truthfully, but my compulsion to ingratiate myself by professing a keen interest for something in which I had no interest won out.

'Absolutely, m'lady. Why?'

'Because my astrologer says we're totally compatible. We're both very

sensitive, feeling, compassionate people.'
'Hey, that's really accurate.'
'Sure. *And it means we can have a depth of sharing and intimacy and emotional union that few others have.'*
'Sounds good.'
'The most amazing thing is that your Venus is in Pisces and so's mine. Plus, your moon is in my 7th house. You know what this means, m'lord?'
'No, what?'
'You're my ideal partner. And I'm yours.'
I wondered what our real horoscope was like.
The one she would have got if she'd used my real date of birth and not the one I'd given her when I'd lied about my age.

 ## Sat 11.17 pm

If Charlotte was going to Sydney, she might just have time to come over and pay me a visit.
During the next couple of IM sessions, I tried to find out as much as I could about the conference.
I had learnt that it lasted for five days and that the itinerary was packed. But then came some promising news. There would be two free days before she had to fly back.
She asked me if I knew of anything she should do while she was in Sydney.
'Well, the harbour is pretty spectacular, and you shouldn't miss Paddington Market. But the one thing I think you should do is come over to Wellington. It's only three hours away.'
'Oh, really? And what's Wellington got?'
'Some fat old twat who really wants to meet you.'
'Fuck me, Sinclair. How could any woman possibly resist?'

 **Fri 6.30 pm**

It was Jacqui's turn to go missing.

She wasn't in the Paris chatroom, so I asked anyone who had seen her recently to privately whisper me.

Within seconds I was contacted by Surferdude.

'Hey, Lord. I was chatting to Lady G maybe a half hour ago. She had to go so's she could meet sumone.'

Before I had time to thank him, Hot Rod whispered that he was currently talking to her on webcam and did I want him to pass on a message?

I didn't. Nor did I want to know that Slayer44 had been playing cards with her earlier. Even worse, he had finished the message with : -)

Dee's_Hair (m) was one of the few males who hadn't seen her, but he wanted me to tell her to call him when I finally did track her down.

I was beginning to think I wasn't the only man in Lady Gwinnivear's life.

Chapter 9

 ## Tue 12.53 pm

It's hard to think about anything else when you have a plastic tube pumping warm water up your arse, but I was wondering if I should tidy up the flat before Charlotte arrived.

This would be a massive undertaking.

While most people count the time since their last proper clean in days, I counted it in years.

Although Lori and I had given the dining room and kitchen a quick dust and polish before the dinner party, every other room hadn't been touched since I moved in.

I had two weeks before Charlotte got here and I reckoned I'd need every minute of that time to make the place presentable.

 ## Thu 12.02 pm

If it hadn't been for the twin temptations of chatrooms and poker, I'm sure I would have had the flat clean in time for Charlotte's arrival.

As it was, I concentrated on the bedroom, in the (as it turned out) misguided belief that she could be persuaded to spend some time there.

As for the rest of the rooms, I ran out of time. I only knew this for certain when I glanced away from the computer to see her plane flying across the hills, beginning its descent to Wellington Airport.

If I couldn't have the flat ready, at least I could get myself ready, so I got in the bath and prepared to meet Charlotte for the first time.

 **Fri 6.44 am**

Something weird happened in the bath.

I washed myself, but then decided I was in no rush to get out. Something in my brain had changed – the part that made me so anxious that I could never bathe longer than a couple of minutes before having to get out.

I'd noticed something similar a couple of times recently, but it hadn't really registered that anything significant was taking place.

I was at the mall and stayed long enough to have a leisurely stroll around the shops instead of rushing around and getting it over as quickly as possible.

A few days later, I sat out in the garden and actually lost track of time. The previous summer, I'd had to force myself to stay out for ten minutes. I had even timed it.

Something good was starting to happen. For the first time, I believed that my illness could be on the way out.

I started to experiment by taking slightly longer journeys than usual and waiting for the panic to overwhelm me.

It never did. Not once.

I was feeling more relaxed. More confident. I even found myself smiling occasionally.

I didn't dare think that I was finally better because I'd thought that too many times.

But today it seemed possible.

What was it all down to?

Sticking a plastic tube up my arse?

Swallowing a cocktail of supplements with names like acidophilus, kelp and Omega-3 every morning?

Having all those fillings taken out?

The colloidal minerals?

Then I realised, it really didn't matter.

🧑 Fri 9.53 am

'Caroline Quentin! It's great to meet you,' I said enthusiastically. 'I've always been a big fan of your work.'

Charlotte stood there in the warm summer rain, two matching yellow suitcases by her side.

'Not funny, Sinclair. Still, good to see you're as fucking unattractive in person as you are on the Internet.'

We both just stood there. I was unsure what to do. Should I give her a peck on the cheek? A full-blown snog? Shake her hand?

I decided on the last and stuck out my hand. She took it, we shook hands formally and I took her bags.

'Come in. I've got some really interesting wallpaper I want you to see.'

She wiped her feet, which was unnecessary, given the state of the floor, and stepped inside.

'Something to drink?' I asked as she sat down on the threadbare chair. 'A cup of herbal tea, perhaps?'

'You remembered!' she exclaimed, looking pleased. 'So what flavours do you have?'

'Well, that's another thing we have in common. I've always loved herbal tea. Been drinking it for years. May I recommend Red Zinger? A refreshing blend of rosehip, hibiscis and…other stuff.'

'Sounds fine.'

Now if I'd let the conversation stop there, I would have got away with it. But I didn't. I completely blew my credibility with the next sentence.

'Milk and sugar?'

She informed me that only a 'complete fuckwit' would put milk into herbal tea. Which did explain why the brew I'd had that morning tasted so disgusting that I had to pour it down the sink.

After that, things got better.

We sat there and talked and talked and talked. It was like a real-life version of an all-day chatroom session, where conversation flows for hours on end and you never want to leave.

I even confessed that I hadn't been entirely truthful about my most embarrassing moment. The one I'd told her about didn't even come close to the time I called my teacher 'Mum' when I was eight years old.

She immediately made me feel better by telling me about the time a customer was leaving the shop and she said, 'Bye. I love you.' She then had to chase after him to explain that she didn't really love him.

By the time the day had passed, I had slowly realised something about Charlotte.

I'd never felt this way about anyone before. And it really was as though we'd known each other our entire lives.

Fri 5.34 pm

After spending all day sitting down, Charlotte wanted to go for a walk.

The thought of this would normally have been enough to bring me out in a cold sweat, reeling off excuses why it was impossible. But two things made it easier.

First, I had nothing to hide. I'd told her everything, so if I did start to get panicky, she'd understand that we would have to rush back.

Second, I'd been making major progress in getting better over the last few weeks. Nothing dramatic, just a slow and steady improvement. I'd even taken a long walk by myself with no ill effects.

It was a beautiful early summer afternoon and I soon discovered that Charlotte's definition of walking differed from mine. Her long, confident strides were in complete contrast to my lethargic shuffling, which meant that every few minutes she had to stop and wait for me to catch up. Apart from that, I was doing well. Thinking back to when leaving the house was a major achievement, I had come a long way. I could now walk past the mall, which I'd honestly thought would never happen again.

I was lost in my thoughts and hadn't realised Charlotte was now so far ahead of me that I couldn't see her. Just as the first signs of anxiety were starting to bubble up, I caught sight of her in the distance and broke into a sort of ungainly jog.

She was waiting for me on the bench that overlooked the bowling green. I sat down beside her, happy to rest my body, which had been pushed to the point of exhaustion.

'Isn't this what old people do?' I said, gasping for breath. 'Sit and watch bowls?'

'We are fucking old, Sinclair,' she said, resting her head on my shoulder.

I tentatively put an arm around her and thought that maybe she had a point.

 Fri 6.10 pm

I was getting used to this going out thing, so suggested we go for a meal at the Casablanca Café.

Charlotte went off to get changed, and reappeared ten minutes later in what she called her 'going out dress'. It was green, long and elegant, and had been designed by someone who was apparently famous, even though I'd never heard of them.

I then noticed that her hair was no longer brown like it was in the photo she'd sent, but a gorgeous, rich burgundy colour.

'I bet Caroline Quentin never looked this good,' I thought to myself.

 Fri 7.03 pm

We sat at the same table that Lori, Cheyenne and I had sat at a lifetime ago. The fire was burning, bathing the room in an orange glow. The difference this time was that I felt relaxed, the conversation was easy and I was with someone I couldn't imagine being without.

I looked across at Charlotte's face, which had mysteriously grown more attractive over the months. Everything was perfect – the lighting, the mood, the timing. Suddenly, I knew what I was going to do.

I asked her to move in with me.

'No.'

'Pardon?'

'I said no, Sinclair. If you want us to be together, you move to Yorkshire. You can give me a hand running the shop.'

'But I can't. I'm not well enough to travel.'

'I don't believe you. You said you weren't well enough to go for a walk, but you seemed fine to me. Besides, I have a life there, and you have no life here. Plus, I've got kids, Sinclair. I can't disrupt their lives. And what would you suggest I do with the shop?'

'Sell it?'

'Do you realise how fucking selfish that is?'

'Yes. Yes, I think I do.'

'So?'

'Well, it's up to you, I suppose.'

'No, Sinclair, it's up to you. You decide. Tell me something – what's my favourite drink?'

'Gin and tonic. Why? Do you want one?'

'No, I want to know how well you know me.'

'I know everything about you. Your favourite song is *Midnight Train to Georgia*, you won medals for archery when you were at school, you've had eight cars, you snore, you started knitting your sister Emily a scarf last year and haven't finished it yet, you only ever eat chocolate when no one else is around – is that enough?'

'So you do listen. Then what the fuck made you think I'd want to throw my life away to move over here? Don't you remember that I once told you I wouldn't change my home for the world?'

'I just thought we were getting on pretty well, and...'She stood up, as though she'd heard enough.

'I'm going back to the hotel now. Look, Sinclair, I don't want to go all tie-a-fucking-yellow-ribbon on you, but if you still want me, you've got my address.'

And with that, she picked up her suitcases and walked out on me.

 ## Fri 8.43 pm

Although I had the car with me, I decided to walk home so that I could let Charlotte's ultimatum sink in. I'd been convinced she'd want to move in with me, and her refusal was a slap in the face. I felt hurt, angry and rejected.

As the house came into sight, I thought of all the other girls who would currently be in the chatroom, and how they compared to the bad-tempered Caroline Quentin lookalike I'd just spent the day with.

For some reason, this didn't make me feel any better.

 Fri 8.56 pm

When I got home I was so distraught that I went straight to bed without even checking my e-mail.

I couldn't believe what had just happened.

She knew I was too ill to travel. Yes, I'd made progress recently, but a journey that long would be my biggest undertaking since my health collapsed.

This wasn't meant to be how it turned out. She was supposed to be so captivated by my charms that she'd want to move in and live happily ever after.

The injustice of it all kept me up most of the night.

 Sat 8.11 am

Next morning, things slowly started to get back to normal. I forced myself out of bed and headed straight for the computer, via the fridge.

I logged on, determined to prove that Charlotte was going to be easy to replace. The chatroom was full of the usual people. There were even three who I'd had cybersex with: BettyBoop33, Pinky_Tuscadero and Lady Gwinnivear. But only one of these had a webcam.

After a brief game of strip poker, things returned to a comfortably predictable state. I was sitting naked, as usual, and I was begging m'lady to show me some of her exotic dance moves, as usual.

As it was my birthday (it wasn't, but she thought it was), she finally relented. Putting on a *Queensryche* song, she started swaying from side to side, tossing her hair back and licking an imaginary ice cream.

I instantly knew why she'd refused to dance for me until now. If she was an exotic dancer, I was a ballerina.

I found myself staring at the screen in disbelief.

Sat 11.17 am

It wasn't Jacqui I was staring at, but myself.

With the webcam program I had, there's a small window on screen that shows the view the other person is getting. I was seeing what she – and every other woman I chatted with – saw.

In my mind, I was a dashing, charming and irresistible lord of the realm, who had a steady stream of lovers.

In reality I was a pale, middle-aged man, badly out of shape, sitting naked in a chair playing with his knob, all alone in a sparsely furnished rented house.

If Jacqui wasn't what she seemed, neither was I.

I suddenly knew what I was going to do.

 # Sun 2.17 am

Booking the flight online took only a couple of minutes. You can get pretty much anything if you have a credit card, computer and modem.

I'd be flying out in six weeks on a direct flight to Heathrow, stopping off at LA for a couple of hours.

Now that I'd paid, there was no going back. But it didn't matter. I'd already made up my mind.

I would rather live in her world than be without her in mine.

 # Sat 8.52 pm

The one rule of online poker that no one had told me was this: it's harder to lose when you're trying to lose than it is to win when you're trying to win.

Outrageous bluffs were working, and senseless gambles were coming off. At one point, I had cyberchips worth over $5000 in front of me, having started out with $765. Slowly but surely, it was whittled away, usually into the hands of a player calling himself Vex, who must have wished I could be there every night.

My last $10 went on a pair of aces, which was no match for Vex's four of a kind.

I double-checked my calculations. In three sessions I was down $1865, which, together with the $2000 for the flight, came to $3865.

The exact sum I'd been planning to lose.

Sat 9.30 pm

Removing the credit card from my wallet, I cut it into tiny pieces and put it in an envelope, addressed to Dave Ferris at the bank.

I then sat down to compose my last letter for him.

Dear Dave,
Thank you for the pre-approved Premier Card. I have spent $3865 on it, which happens to be the exact amount you got out of paying me when I left the bank.
Yours,
Trevor Niblock

One of the advantages of working for the same bank that issued my credit card was knowing that they never took legal action to recover debts of less than $5000 – so there was little chance of them bothering to track me down.

Chapter 10

 Tue 9.14 am

I took the bus into town, which was something I hadn't done since the days of padded shoulders and Rubik's Cube.

The idea was to buy myself all the things I'd need to take with me to West Yorkshire. I was going to leave all the remnants of my reclusive, loveless life behind. They belonged to a different time.

It was winter where I was going, but I thought it best to travel light. A few essentials, such as sweaters, a couple of pairs of jeans and some presents for Charlotte and the kids.

It would be a completely fresh start.

I'd given four weeks' notice on the flat, telling the landlord (who had shown no interest in my plans) that I was moving to the UK to live with my girlfriend.

Flushed with excitement at the prospect of starting over, I'd put a few of the more valuable items I owned up on eBay. What didn't go there, I gave to the Salvation Army, including a large bag of freshly washed women's underwear. And what they didn't want, I threw away.

Letting go of the computer was the hardest thing. It had given me a life when I might otherwise have given up. But it had to go. I was interested to see how much I'd be able to get for it, but I was going to sell it whatever it was worth.

Walking into the computer shop was almost as hard as walking out of the front door had been ten years earlier.

Dave Roberts

 **Fri 10.21 am**

The taxi was waiting outside.

I checked I had everything, then left that ghastly flat for the last time and climbed into the cab. The driver looked at me suspiciously, remembering that I'd once made him turn back after a short distance and a full-blown panic attack.

Today, I was a different person.

'The airport, please,' I said. 'And don't worry, mate. This time, I'm really going.'

I sat back, feeling more relaxed and excited than I'd felt for many, many years, taking in Wellington's sights as we drove through town in plenty of time to catch the flight that was taking me to my new life.

All I had with me was a bag containing a few clothes and gifts. And my new, Internet-ready laptop, which was clutched to my chest.